Queen of
no Tomorrows

Broken Eye Books is an independent press, here to bring you the odd, strange, and offbeat side of speculative fiction. Our stories tend to blend genres, highlighting the weird and blurring its boundaries with horror, sci-fi, and fantasy.

Support weird. Support indie.

brokeneyebooks.com

twitter.com/brokeneyebooks
facebook.com/brokeneyebooks

Queen of No Tomorrows

MATT MAXWELL

QUEEN OF NO TOMORROWS
by MATT MAXWELL
Published by
Broken Eye Books
www.brokeneyebooks.com

978-1-940372-35-8 (trade paperback)
978-1-940372-37-2 (ebook)

MATT
MAXWELL

DEDICATION

For my wife Jennifer, who insisted the world would come around.

QUEEN OF
NO TOMORROWS

ﾑAIT TRIED TO BIND THE PAGES, BUT THE BOOK SLIPPED AWAY FROM HER. She cursed and snapped back, steadying herself before pulling the pages tight with a steady draw on the ligature.

Tired. Too tired.

She caught the scent of them once more, sweet vanilla faded into bitter ash. The smell of the pages *suggested* age; the snap and brittle crinkle of the texture fully convinced her. She held before her something older than any living person, if not legitimately ancient. A lost book, stolen back from obscurity by her and her alone.

She flipped the manuscript over to the blank flyleaf. Not precisely blank yet bare of any visible writing. Color and texture blended, imperfect and rough. In the near-absence of content lay the suggestion of it, half-erased scratches of ink faded to lines the color of rust or dried blood. Stare at it long enough and anyone could have been convinced of its importance. Of course it meant something. Of course the obliterated text was crucial. Of course it wasn't a trap that appealed to ego and vanity.

The emperor's new clothes aren't clothes at all. Nobody wants to be shown up as a fool, to admit that they were taken in. So they'll make their own mythology, get tangled up in it rather than admit that there was nothing there.

The suggestive nearly blank worked better than a mind trap. And if it didn't, then the artistry of the frontispiece did. A veil of aggregated eyes, each iris different from the rest, hung in the space between the stars. The vision seemed to be caught in mid-dissolution, dust and mist wisping away as if no longer allowed to exist. A pair of hands framed it all: human in proportion, though elongated and with palms extended to the viewer. On the right, a perfectly formed but only half-opened eye gazed back from beneath the fingers. On the left lay a mouth, lips parted to show teeth and pulled back at the corners in a smile of chilling indifference.

Cait couldn't have told you where any of this had come from. She'd drawn the work, aged the paper, scented the pages, worked together the whole of it, making the codex real. Nearly . . .

But where it had come from? She could talk about it until exhaustion and not know its origin. She knew, though, that the *Smoking Codex* was her work. Without her, it wouldn't have existed.

She'd copied and forged books before, good enough to fool professors, enemies, and even friends. For a little while at least. Vivian might never speak to her again, and Cait should have known that she'd never stand for forgeries. Cait, however, made copies and fakes and pulled down enough doing it to feel less than bad.

Still, she'd never been brave enough to make one of her own.

Not just a scribe but a creator. Not a copyist but an artist.

Cait stared at the frontispiece, lost in the swirls of dust and matter like a star being torn to vapor, making the border between something and nothing impossible to discern. She stared into it, unable to remember precisely drawing this, but who else could have? Here it lay before her in the pool of light on the desk, strung together by her own hands and made real but driven by an unnamed outside force, one free from the bounds of consciousness or conscience. The *Smoking Codex* was a testament to an unreal god or being willing themself into existence. Cait's fictional provenance for the piece declared it written by the last of the religion's surviving adherents, confessed to an invader who couldn't understand the primal beauty and raw truth but who would be cursed to carry this word back to civilization.

A good story. Who could resist this? Nobody. The same men who paid top dollar for copies of the Darrab Althtaeban *surely would pay even more for something that nobody else could possibly claim to own. They thought the having of it conferred power, brought on by mere possession.*

It would just take some time to build up the legend. Feed the name around and let the whispering campaign do the hard work for me.

She traced the lines of the fingers on the page before her, counting out the extra joints on one, the extra digits on the other, neither of them quite human. *Maybe too beautiful to let go of so easily.*

Then the fear clutched at her. Would it even be accepted? Would it be loved for its own beauty or just lusted after for the promise of ancient power on its pages? It had no reputation, forbidden or otherwise, to fall back upon. That had to be built. And even then, Cait could take no credit for it, a thing that she thought she could get used to but that turned out to be self-delusion. The thought of creation itched in her. She could push that urge away for a time, but it always returned to bite twice as hard as before. Always.

She looked over at the cover on the drying stand. The book it once housed had been scavenged from an estate sale for a tiny fraction of its real value. No collector in their right mind would want such a thing, cracked and ravaged by neglect or moisture or sunlight. Worthless but perfect for conveying age and the authority that came with it. Once covered and the gluing sufficiently distressed to match, the codex would be done. Not even an afternoon's work. Finished.

A part of her shied away at that. If it were done, she'd have to let it go. She would—

The phone's ring shrilled, and Cait started.

I could just go to work and let this drop. They'll call again if it's important.

She grabbed the handset from the green-black plastic phone, splattered with ink and paint so that the numbers on the rotary dial were all but unreadable now.

"What."

"Roja. Roja, it's me."

"When are you going to stop calling me that, Rico?"

"The twelfth of never."

Her hair was only partly red today with bold streaking on black like bright blood over asphalt. It had taken the better part of an afternoon a week ago and who knew how much experimentation on Trace's part to get the colors to do what they did. Cait's boss at the library had turned white with anger at the change, which Trace still laughed at. Nobody saw her down in the stacks or in restoration, just how she liked it. Where it was quiet. No attention.

"It's not all red today." She flipped the cover off the rack and set it over the bound manuscript, checking the fit. "Now what do you want that you finally call after hiding the hell out for a week? I was worried about you."

"I'm fine. You don't need to worry about me." He drew a hesitant breath, fluttering on the line. "Now I want you to sit down. This is big."

"Speaking of big, you gotta come over and pick up these books for this Khan guy, if that's even his real name."

"Well it's sorta about that." His voice became sweet and slippery now. "We've got a new client."

"*I* don't need new clients, Rico. I need to make sure the ones who are lined up are taken care of. Khan is getting grouchy, and you're supposed to see him in, like, five hours." That was a guess, but lighting a fire under Rico usually gave results.

"I can't go."

Cait took the phone, tapped it on the desk twice, and said, "This thing must be broken. You just said that—"

"I'm sorry, Roja, but I have to tender this."

"Khan knows *you* not me. I've never even talked to him. And what the hell is this other deal you're so wound up about?"

"Just . . . you have to trust me on this one. It's big."

"Trust is saying you'll do a thing, not punk out and leave me doing the sale. Or having to call my goddamn sister to bail me out because you chose to disappear when I really needed you there. You remember that, right?" She regretted saying the words even as they screamed away down the phone line. Too late to take back now.

Rico's dry swallow echoed, "Don't talk about that shit again. It's settled, and you made that call, not me." His voice had dropped to acid and dismissal, and it made her feel three inches tall. "I'm talking about tall dollars here. And they asked for you by name."

"You mean they asked for Rory Soame, and big fat deal, that name is finally getting around."

It had taken long enough. More than a year with a man's name on the letterhead to get replies from book dealers. Who the hell knew how Vivian had done it, especially with her circumstances.

"No, baby. They asked for *you*. Not by name but like they were reading a rap sheet and—"

Cait sat up very straight now, wired to the chair. "Shut up. Nobody knows who the hell I am."

"They did. She did."

"Who the hell are you talking about?" She let slip her anger and irritation at him for weaseling out. He'd always done that when the hammer was about to fall.

There was something else though, anger at the interruption. Things were so close and being held up now by this. Her finger traced one of the eyes, nail biting hard enough to scratch the paper. Another scar for an old page.

"The queen, baby."

"Who?"

He laughed. It edged up to drunkenness, and Cait bit her tongue at the thoughts that brought. "You'll have to meet her. This is the big time. Biggest." Something flared behind his words, a flush of greedy blood.

Cait's breath sucked in, ragged over her teeth. "Are you high again? You fucking *promised*."

"Ain't your business anymore, even if I was," he said with a sneer. "Remember? Just business. And I brought it up. You should thank me."

"You son of a bitch!"

"Maybe, but I'm the son of a bitch who's making us a ton of money."

"And what about the deal you're hanging me to dry on? That's today."

"That's *your* today. Your tomorrow is bigger, thanks to me. This deal is going to pull us ten thousand. Maybe more. See, they got that light of the believer in their eyes. They want this bad."

"Which book? You got a name?" She was trying to pin this down at least. The talk about believers got her nervous. Most everyone in the business picked these books over, like academics and scam artists trying to uncover a new angle. Wasn't a one of them that really read into it for deeper truth. Until you found those who did, and she'd done everything she could to dodge that crowd.

"They didn't say, just that only you would have it."

"You're being fishy."

"Sure, Cait. I'm also hungry, you know?" His voice bit. "You've been holding our thing back, and I just stepped it out some. I'm doing what you said you wanted. Now quit worrying about it, and let things happen."

"That's a terrible plan. And it's not ours, it's *mine*. I get the books. Hell, I make them."

"And they're worth whatever someone will pay. Why are you taking a shit on my part of this? Without clients, you're just a collector." He jabbed the last word.

"Knock it off. I won't see anyone I don't know."

"Then you'll meet. They'll contact us later, and I'll help seal the deal."

Something nipped at her. She wrote it off as sleeplessness or hunger. She'd been working most of the night, thinking the day hers to sleep away. With that gone, the prospect of being out in the world was just too much.

"Rico," she started.

"Baby, trust."

The words were warm and soothing in her ears, imagining his arm around her at the back door of the club. It had been cold that night but not when she had been by him.

"You make it hard to." Between getting high and the trouble he flirted with, that trust had frayed to threads long ago.

"It'll pay off. And don't worry about Khan. He's a pussycat. Look, these cats want the book. Nothing else. No danger in it. No Tomorrows is just rep and—" He hung there.

"What did you say?"

"Nothing. I didn't say anything."

"Don't jerk me around. You said 'No Tomorrows.' You just tried to bury it."

"I said we'll be fine when this is done."

She felt sick and laid that at the feet of being up all night, not the name that had dropped. "No. There isn't 'fine.' Not with them. That's not in your control."

"Neither is the rain. We'll talk later, Roja."

That last word came out sweet, and it had almost always worked on her. It could've this time if she let it. That nibbling unease bit down harder as she hung up the phone.

No Tomorrows ran a lot of trouble into downtown and out through Hollywood. Even if their reputation was just paper-thin and overblown, it still ran a shudder through Cait. It wasn't just the violence of their actions but the creativity and disregard they ran with. They played at something other than mere crime. Every group or gang or whatever you wanted to call them, they had to have a gimmick, an identity. Even if it was just pretend, just pretend magic. But what No Tomorrows pretended to made her think three times about this deal.

And gangs been killing other gangs since before Dad was a kid here. Doesn't make any sense, but that doesn't stop it from happening. But they're not even that. They don't have a block or a territory. They just roam like smoke and are harder to catch.

The rain outside finally let down. Over the LA basin, the lead-heavy skies dropped rain big as bullets, a monsoonal force capable of washing every street clean as sure as a tuxedo car flicking its searchlight and scattering an alley. No Tomorrows though, they'd stand there and invite the cops to step out.

The smart ones wouldn't.

⌇

The sidewalk ahead of her was littered with countless dead worms, dried up and curled into a scattering of epileptic punctuation. The rain drew or drowned them out last night, only to wither up in the sunshine.

Cait looked up without need to shade her eyes as the clouds moved between her and the sun. They closed around it in a slow swarming, feeling like something alive.

The fingers opened again and sunlight poured down on Melrose Drive, and the light beside her at Highland turned green. Cars jumped at the signal, engines roaring in a reflexive frenzy.

Of going nowhere.

Her heels scuffed to a stop on the sidewalk, and she scanned the signage on the store marquees, all different styles, all hovering around readability, but forgoing it for fashion. The facades around her were still bright and clean. Trendy boutiques on this strip often didn't last long enough to get grimy and sun-beaten before going out of business and having something fresher step into the old skin. The neon sign of a shoe store buzzed next to her, glow all but invisible in the daytime, only a faint blue trace around the tube. It sounded like a big insect trapped behind the glass, monotone and tireless.

Cait adjusted the bundle of books under her arm as she reached for the backpack that wasn't there.

Right. Purse. I'm a grownup today.

And while she wasn't a punk any more, she wasn't too far removed.

I'm the featured attraction this afternoon, so dress for the right kind of scrutiny. Let 'em stare. Brains are disengaged while eyes are digging in.

Which was why Cait dressed her best today. She wore a black pencil skirt cut just below the knees, stockings sheer enough to show expectedly pale skin but fading to a pleasant contrast at glancing angles. Her cream-colored blouse fit well enough to be a distraction when she allowed it. Now it was well hidden beneath a dark maroon leather jacket. Her glasses were off for the moment but would come on for business. A silly and stupid thing perhaps, but whatever put her target at ease, Cait would do. It was one thing to be an undergraduate with unruly and dyed hair, ripped up jeans, and high-tops on the wrong side of the grave. Another to be dressed like that at a sale. And she would have to do enough explaining as to why Rico wasn't there, so no Savage Republic or Siouxsie shirts today.

Misdirect. Or rather, direct to what you want the buyer to see, not what's there.

She read the address and checked again: Squared Water, Melrose and North Mansfield.

How many aquarium shops can there be on Melrose anyway?

Cait hoped there weren't going to be any decapitated bombshells along the way.

She shifted the books back to her left side. They were all of different sizes, making a sort of rough and flat ziggurat underneath the black cloth that held them. Of the three, two were authentically old: a 1928 edition of *The Unseen Sun* and an 1865 translation of *Darrab Althtaeban*. The smallest of the books, a copy of *The Source of Shadow*. It was indeed a copy, but she doubted even the original transcriber, Broken Moon himself, could have recognized it as such.

A cloth wrapped the slim volume, one rubbed in coal ash and camphor and crushed roses as had the pages themselves. The treatment of the work invited expectation and could also defuse skepticism. Presentation was everything.

Cait slipped her glasses on, black-rimmed and subtly tapered, and pushed open the door to the place. Right on time.

The sunlight fell dead inside the store. Instead, purplish aquarium light lit everything, filtered through the hundreds of tanks stretching back into the reaches of the place. The hum of air pumps and quietly bubbling water rippled, surrounding her. Between the sound and the watery light, the store felt small and closed in as a submarine. It smelled halfway between reptile house and low tide, making her face wrinkle in reflex.

"May I help you?" asked a gangly man with his arm in a tank up to his elbow, waving his submerged hand. He looked past her, his eyes adjusting to the sliver of daylight she'd let in.

"Yes, I'm meeting someone here," Cait said. "Mister, ah, Khan. I was told to be expected." She approached the tank, unable to see its contents due to her angle.

"He's in the back by the saltwater tropicals." The man turned his head atop his neck to the point of hyperextension, jutting out his sharp and unshaven chin.

In the light, he looked like one of those underwater idols she'd seen off Cyprus or Greece maybe, drowned nobility. He moved his hand in the tank again, releasing tatters of white junk to the water. On the sandy floor of the tank, a nearly invisible slug or blob extended translucent and amorphous lips, pattering over his fingertips and eating what he held.

Cait caught herself staring at it.

"Don't make a face now," he said. "It's just a nudibranch."

The thing sucked in the pseudo-mouth and inched forward. Though mostly translucent, at the right angles, it glowed a white-purple in the tank light, like a jellyfish in moonbeams.

"People keep these as pets?"

"A select few." He smiled like he knew what that meant. "Go on back. Khan's waiting."

He went back to feeding the thing, whatever it was, as Cait crossed through the shop. She passed walls of glass, each one a miniature world pinned behind it. She tried to remember what Rico had said about Khan a couple weeks ago, as the buyer and seller orbited one another, slowly drawing in.

This guy's a swindler. Just like me. Selling the best possible futures to anyone made hungry from doubt. Lots of housewives on the Westside and maybe the mistresses who went with their husbands too. Probably playing one off the other.

His cologne greeted her before he could, even with the ocean smell trying to smother it. She turned a corner into a daylight-bright alcove, and he stood before a bank of glass. Brazenly painted fish lazed on the other side like idling, underwater hot rods waiting at a starting light. He stood, staring into the tanks, making them feel deeper than they were.

Fake sunlight seemed to radiate from every wall. The thought of how the fake would read in this weird light flashed through Cait's mind, but she put it aside just as quickly. Some clients could smell this sort of even momentary hesitation, and she wished again that Rico was doing this. He read people so well, so easily.

He always had.

"Ah, mister—" Khan started to say as he turned and stopped, eyes fixed on Cait. He swept them up and down the length of her, taking the space of several long breaths to do so. "Well this is a pleasant surprise." He extended a hand with expectation and held it there. Silver rings stood out against tanned skin.

She glanced him over quickly. He wore a blue Nehru jacket of once fine but now going tatty wool with matching pants. A white, silk pocket square looked like a tiny ship's sail, folded to three points on the sea of his breast. His had a deep California tan, wrinkles at his eyes and neck, stretching his age from anywhere between thirty and fifty. A dark karakul hat perched precariously on his head, begging to be tipped the rest of the way off. Around his neck hung a long, polished bronze chain with a crooked chunk of shiny black stone as long as a man's thumb as a pendant. Vaguely Eastern European mystic in bearing, "exotic" enough to thrill the marks he no doubt surrounded himself with. The dark and earthy musk of his cologne clung too close in the room.

He coughed once and wiggled his fingers as if to take her hand to, of course, kiss. Cait brought her right hand in low, held to shake.

Khan smirked at this and took another look at her. "Where is your . . . associate Rico? I'd thought I'd be meeting him." His gray eyes crinkled up as he smiled disarmingly.

She took the hand and found it at least dry.

"Family emergency. Mister Soame has sent me instead. I hope that isn't a problem."

"Most assuredly not." He winked.

Cait coughed to keep from laughing.

"Such a lovely assistant," he resumed with a warm and oily charm. "One wonders why Soame would ever allow you leave his library."

Because I invented him, you moron.

She instead flashed a smile and went grave. "His condition prevents him from leaving his house during daylight hours." She looked for a place to stand the books at least but found nothing besides fish and more fish.

"So he's an actual 'moonchild' is he? Awful business. Never seeing the sun? Like a vampire."

As if such a thing existed. Though porphyria was real enough and would keep an eccentric inside and away from direct human contact. No golf games or lunch meetings for him.

Cait tried to place his accent but couldn't. Part Scottish, part Midwestern perhaps. She guessed she wasn't getting the full treatment.

"Mr. Soame gets by. He's able to accomplish quite a lot from his study by phone and computer now." More comforting lies.

"With the help of his lovely assistant, I'm sure." He winked again, and Cait wanted to punch him in that eye.

"You're too kind."

"Not hardly enough. And such amazing hair." Khan reached out to touch it, and Cait sidestepped at the last second.

"Is there a table or anything like that here?" She glanced around. "You'll be wanting to examine the books."

His eyes waited for hers to come to them. "Of course. May I?" Bronzed hands unfolded before her, revealing surprisingly pinkish palms. They waited as she drew the moment out.

She pulled at one of the corners of the black cloth and let it fall away from the books, their scent lost to the rancid seawater, and she sank at that. The *Darrab Althtaeban* being the largest, she passed it along to him first.

"Mr. Soame apologizes, but the source for the 1847 version is being . . . finicky now. This was the oldest he could secure. The Labyrinth Press edition from Boston, 1888."

He drew himself up as he took the book from her. "This is the more beautiful edition anyway," he said and waved his free hand like shooing away a fly. "Superior construction technique and clearly the more desirable."

Then why did you ask for the 1872, you big fake?

The texture of the cover was rough, an artifact of the size of the light source in the room. He turned the book over in his hands but brought it no closer.

Maybe he isn't entirely an idiot. This isn't library light, but it might be enough to spot the fake.

She watched him eating up the volume with his eyes.

At least it's not me for the moment.

"'The Trail of the Serpent,' in English," he said and looked at her, awaiting confirmation of his erudition.

"*Very* impressive," Cait replied, crinkling her nose just a little. "The writing's of unknown origin, finally codified by the Ottoman scholar Naith Fahim, who had to flee the empire for Paris after being revealed as a *she* rather than a *he*. This volume is said to translate the tracks of the desert creatures into secrets that humans long ago lost. Utmost forbidden."

Cait smiled and waited.

Khan paused, looked up from the book with a flat smirk and watched her with interest. "There's more to you than the dye and glasses, isn't there?"

"Always," she replied. "Speaking of more. I have a line on something new and, frankly, a book I've only heard whispers of."

He grunted. "And what did Mr. Soame think?" He snapped the first book closed and peered into her.

"Mister Soame set me to track the story down. A book called the *Smoking Codex*."

"And?" He tapped his foot twice and simmered.

"A translation of the teachings of a post-Mayan scholar and—"

He waved the rest of the sentence away. "New world magic. Worthless."

"The summoning and binding of the Servant of Dust," Cait tried to add.

His eyes were dead. Worse, they were bored. "Something I asked for, please. My time is valuable, and you waste it with this."

She held her bile instead of spitting it at him. "Certainly. *The Source of Shadow*? I believe you asked after this one in particular."

"That's better." He rocked back on his heels and let out a thin smile.

She stood for a moment and withdrew the smallest volume with some deliberate ceremony, holding it before him balanced on her palm, inviting him to unwrap it. He brought it up to his face. The smell of the perfumed cloth, warmed and released by her touch, would hit him even in competition with the aquarium stink.

"Go ahead," she urged.

He pulled the cloth aside, deep wine in color. The light in his eyes told her that she'd already won. Men could scarcely protect themselves from the desire in their hearts. The challenge lay only in feeding them the familiar, teasing out the thing they were really after.

Give the client what they want even if it's fake.

His fingers trembled slightly at touching the book, lingering on the cover in the faux-tropical glow.

"A calfskin cover, tanned by moonlight. The rumors are true."

Calfskin, yes, but otherwise quite ordinary. No need to ruin his good time with facts.

She watched as his fingers stopped. He quickly withdrew them, inhaling sharply. He stood up as if on puppet strings, and his eyes went back to boring into her.

"Tell me—" he said and stopped, lips pulled hard back over his teeth, so hard that Cait thought they would split.

Her pulse jumped, but she let the shock pass through her, rolling with the punch.

Khan sucked in a breath. "You must tell me where you obtained this." His eyes tried to drill down into her.

I bet Betty from Bel Air melts at this. You'll have to do better with me.

"Do you really care where it came from?" she asked. She slipped the cloth back over the slim volume, disappearing it. "Or do you care that it's in front of you now? Mister Soame asks me a question every time I ask about provenance."

"And that is?"

"'What story do you want to hear, my dear?'" She brought the book away from him, watching Khan wrestle with himself as if a boy, holding onto a boy's dream for a moment and watching it being taken away.

Though immovable and cool on the outside, she clenched her teeth at the insult.

This fool is willing to take the word of a man who doesn't exist over that of a woman standing in front of him.

She'd been served this sort of pigheadedness since she could remember, but it never got easier to deal with. No matter how much more she learned than her teachers, she was always beneath consideration.

Her contempt sublimated, radiating from her like dry ice fog. "If this is not satisfactory, other buyers are waiting. And your time is valuable as is mine."

She tapped her foot twice, crisp and sharp.

The stone face softened to clay, and he smiled, showing ivory-white teeth expertly capped. "Please. You have to understand." He reached for words that slipped through his fingers. "I, of course, will pay the agreed-upon price."

You sure will.

She would spend the money on a new dye job, making it just a little sweeter without Rico's cut.

At least until she simmered and thought about Khan's dismissal of the codex. She wasn't supposed to take it personally, bad for business.

But she couldn't *not* think about it as she rode across town. It was all imaginary bullshit anyway, right? Why seek one book over another, just because it had been referred to by others or came from a certain place.

She'd work on the codex more, keep up the whispering campaign.

ﺤ

The strip mall off Glendale Boulevard, a low, stucco affair, glowed with electric signage in the slanting daylight. Somewhere on the other side of the hills, the Silver Lake Reservoir glinted, a precious jewel keeping the residents in showers and clean driveways. Cait stood in front of the glass doorway, through which a stylized sign burned with the name Distress in spiky, angular type.

"Boy trouble? You look it." Trace asked. She finished a long draw on her cigarette, dropped it, and ground it out. Ratty jeans clung to her skinny but muscular frame, and she wore a half shirt that said "I Don't Care" in solid block letters.

"No," Cait said. "Well yes. But not one specific one."

"Boys are a mess. Since forever ago, girl." Her platinum hair caught the purple-pink from the neon, even in the last sunlight. "You should give 'em up. Life gets easier that way."

"Men are easy enough to deal with." She sighed hard. "Business partners are another thing."

Trace exhaled two thin streams of smoke and smiled. "Mm-hmm. Especially if you've ever slept with them."

Cait let the pained grimace come. "Long time ago."

"Mm-hmm." Her fingers reached out and ran through Cait's hair. "Now what do you want to do with all this? Bored already? Not getting enough attention?"

"I was thinking just a purple wrap." Cait waited for the fingers to come free. "Like I'm always in this neon glow here, maybe."

"We can do that if you really want to *pay* for it. But over the black? You make it hard."

"Not the first time I've heard that."

Trace smirked but only a little. "Let's get you in the chair. Lay back, and you can tell me all your secrets."

Rinsed and lathered before she knew it, Cait's tension melted away under Trace's strong fingers, insistent but never pushy as they worked over her scalp.

"Tell me there's a man that makes you feel this good."

"Never found a man who offered to wash my hair. That's not what they're after."

They always wanted something and didn't care how they got it. Even Rico after a while. Maybe always.

Cait pushed the thought away, but it stuck with cactus thorns. Rico had been crazy and kind at first, and she just watched him turn it off the same way he'd turned it on when they met at Halfway Gone years back. Eight years. Five months.

They'd hung out in the gallery and made fun of the college kids who'd come by mistake or the Palos Verdes chumps looking to score. He'd had such pretty, dark eyes, still did, but they never flashed for Cait anymore. He'd moved on. Pity that, since he still had enough good contacts and she had enough good books to move, they did better together than permanently apart. And he'd always pushed to sell to anyone with money, not just collectors.

Even crooks. He knew a few.

"You look lost, girl."

The smell of the hair dye and ashtrays and cooling Mexican food in Styrofoam trays snapped Cait right back. Her eyes opened, almost disappointed to have Trace looming over her, wrists deep in suds and warm water.

"Yeah, I just need to get him to pick up, 'specially after this last message. Won't even answer his calls." She swung her eyes to Trace's and asked, "You think he'd use a phone? One of those mobile jobs?"

"Only criminals and movie stars and the lawyers who service them can afford those things. Besides, that boy will buck a leash straight off." Trace half-smiled, letting the diamond in her front tooth glitter. "Sit back down, and don't worry about what can't be controlled. I'll be running the color after we rinse off here."

Warm water rippled over Cait's scalp, and she sank back into the chair, forgetting everything else besides the sensation of letting go.

"Final check. Amethyst Nightshade, right? Geez, who names this stuff?"

"Failed English majors." Cait opened her eyes to the bottle of purple pigment so close she couldn't see anything else clearly. "Yeah. Just so long as it doesn't turn out *that* dark."

"It's all gonna be almost invisible on top of that black, honey. But it'll show in the sunlight real good." Trace snapped on a latex glove. "Now cough."

"Don't you dare," Cait growled.

"Never without permission."

The bitter dye smell swept all around Cait, strong enough to take it in even through her mouth. She gritted her teeth and breathed through them.

"Smells like chemistry lab."

"Only for the next couple hours. So stay put. Maybe a nap. You look like you could use it."

At the suggestion, Cait could barely stay awake.

Trace likes to flirt, but it's all talk.

She closed her eyes and imagined her long hair in the sun with highlights glowing. Anyone could bleach and go bright purple, and she saw it all the time at the club. Hair as fuck-you, which got old even for her.

I'll just check on Rico and get back to work on the codex. Then figure out what to do with it. And his new clients.

Swirls of hair lingered behind her eyes, billowing like smoke from the surface of the obsidian mirror. She thought of the finished pages. But then what? The whole thing had been an indulgence, just a chance to do something that spoke to her, not to make a prize sought by someone else, another thing to control or to seek control with.

But would anyone want this?

The *Darrab Althtaeban* had been a good copy but only that. A copy. One good enough to make Mr. Khan roll over and show his belly, but it was empty work. Familiar pieces or rote duplication. No room for expansion, just a frozen re-creation.

The *Smoking Codex* was something else. It breathed. Once she'd understood the book, the codex wrote itself, images came to her mind even as she slept. It breathed through her. She ran her fingers through the book, the text of it, like through a tiger's fur. Another life roared beneath them, thrilling.

The scrape of metal door frame on tile knifed her in the ear. She kept her reaction to a pair of clenched hands.

"Lay on back down, girl," Trace breathed. "Company's here." Whatever humor there might've been in her words vanished like gasoline on a hot day.

Cait did as told, still not quite sure if she'd been dreaming. She opened her eyes as much as she could without revealing she was awake.

Two people had stepped through the door already, a man and a younger woman. The man was maybe Cait's height in heels, a dancer's build sculpted in red clay, his black shirt tight over his chest. The shop lights gleamed in his street-elegant pompadour, highlights cut like record grooves, conforming to every contour of his skull as he scanned the room. Silver hoops hung from his left ear, pierced all the way along its outer edge.

He stopped at the doorway and pulled what looked like a multifaceted icicle of faintly colored glass from a sheath on his hip. He carved a shape out of the air, letting a faint look of satisfaction play over his lips before he replaced the blade and stepped forward to one side. A familiarity in the gesture spoke to Cait, but its message was unclear.

The woman with him wore her long, black hair tied back into two braids that looped back into one another, nooses against the texture of her leather coat. Sunglasses wrapped around her eyes, blanking out identity. Her skin was a rich brown, darker but less red than her partner's, not a Malibu suntan as Khan's had been.

Cait's gaze rested on the woman's mouth. Instead of lipstick, she had four black *X*'s drawn in a row across them. At first glance, Cait almost thought they'd been sewn shut and couldn't believe it. The woman's features were strong and unbending, her bearing no less firm. Hers was a line that went back before Columbus, much further; it was ancient in a place where old meant fifty years, a different understanding of time and one that wouldn't be bent. Her gaze stopped at Trace, and she smiled. Cait went cold for her.

"Good evening," Trace growled. "Here for a cut? I can do that."

The woman said nothing for the space of several heartbeats.

Cait's eyes passed over the pair again. Tattoos swarmed over his arms from his bicep all the way to the backs of his hands, even his neck. At a distance, they made the as little sense as the graffiti on a liquor store wall. He crossed his arms before him and showed the spiderweb tattoo on the back of his hand with an unmistakable black widow at the center. Above that, there were a stylized *N* and *T* intertwined, legs like snakes joined in copulation. A half-closed eye marked his other hand, the same letters conjoined. He turned his hip for a moment, and the cold light of a carelessly open straight razor gleamed below a belt loop.

Trace's insult bounced off the woman like she was carved from a cliff face. She lifted her left hand, the one marked with that same spider, holding it a few inches from her face before she spoke, obscuring her lips as she did so.

"No Tomorrows keep their own time." Her voice sounded distinct and clear, even with the hand over it. "Though your joke was very funny." She lowered her hand with some ceremony.

Shivers went up Cait's arms at the name. Though a draft came from the open door, still afternoon warm, their reputation chilled her, stories of murders and worse, paths crossed at clubs and on the street. Not just the fear of reputation but knowing how it had been earned in unsolved crimes and members who never managed to end up locked away. They were magic like that.

The man pulled a pair of scissors from a tangle of them stuffed into a glass jar. He opened and balanced it on his palm, not looking as he did so.

Cait imagined a tiny cut there but couldn't see it.

"You're a long way from your territory," Cait said finally. "Important business?" She kept her fingers on the worn vinyl armrest to keep herself grounded. The cracks and seams blown out from wear were reassuring and real beneath her skin.

"Everywhere is our territory."

Trace hissed at Cait, fingers pressed into her shoulders. "Shut your mouth. My place. I got this."

Equally harsh, Cait whispered back "You'll just piss them off."

Trace's fingers squeezed Cait's shoulder. "Fine. All yours."

The woman watched the exchange, eyes still erased behind the smoked lenses, but her gaze spearing into Trace. "You should smoke yourself to cancer. Outside."

"My friend—" Trace snapped.

"Is in no danger. Or we would have been cleaning up and leaving already."

Cait wanted to believe that but couldn't dismiss the cold blood down her neck so easily. Club memories slipped back, populated with black-clad kids with cold faces. They never danced, only moving through the place like a haunted house ride, punks and weirdos flowing around them without making eye contact, even the hardest ones. They never paid for drinks and got whatever they wanted.

And sometimes people died for it anyways.

"I'll be just outside," Trace said.

"Don't worry. I'll be fine," Cait repeated Rico's lie.

Trace's heels scraped over the tile floor, forcing her to move around the pair to escape the salon.

"Relax," the woman said as her hand came down, fingers dancing briefly in the transit. "That will be a wicked purple when it's done. Would be a shame to make a mess with it. Lie back."

The words weighed on Cait like summer heat. She didn't think she could get up even if the chair were on fire.

"Who are you?" she asked. Her own voice sounded thin and reedy by comparison.

She raised her hand again so that Cait could only see the tattoos. "I am Alondra," she said, still clearly even though obscured. Liquid gold from the sunset poured over her features, impervious to time. "And my sister, the queen, has business with you."

"I'm not going anywhere."

Alondra didn't hear the refusal. "Not tonight, no." She leaned against the pastel-painted counter and pointed toward Cait. "You are a difficult woman to get hold of."

"I'm in the book."

Cait could hear the leather jacket shrug. "That's not what I meant. We had to work some."

"Bullshit. Rico led you to me." She felt something warm and shameful shoot through her. More than that, Rico had betrayed a trust, cutting deep.

"But *something* had to lead us to Mr. Cisneros." She left the riddle unanswered.

"Your money got to him." The slice of his betrayal gushed out over Cait's insides. "Or was it cheap dope?"

Alondra watched her, twin nooses of hair hanging glossy and lustrous and strong. The face under the wraparound shades offered no judgment.

"And why isn't he here?" Cait sat up and felt the slap of her hair falling onto the poncho and winced. Purple goop must have been running down her back now. "He's supposed to be here."

She replied with a cool, "He isn't important. We're here to see you."

"Success. Now stop wasting my time." Cait could hear the dye dripping from her hair to the floor in the silence as she waited.

Alondra's glasses stared from above the back of her hand. "The queen wishes to arrange a meeting. Tomorrow. Nine o'clock at the Last Prayer Club on Cherokee. You know it."

Something had happened to her voice, but Cait couldn't understand what. It was a dry whisper into Cait's ear, but the distance between them made that inconceivable. She wrestled with the riddle of it and every answer made her more uncertain. It sounded as if it had come across years uncounted instead of simply crossing the dingy, neon-glow salon.

"Yes. But it's not my kind of place."

"Oh? You're missing out. But you'll be rewarded when you come tomorrow night."

"Not if?"

"The queen does not talk about conditions. She wants your book." Alondra's voice showed irritation now, a sandpaper roughness at its edges. Whether that tone was for the queen or for Cait was unclear.

"Which one? I've got a library's worth."

"The *Smoking Codex*."

The floor under the chair gave way for an instant, and Cait had to pull herself back. Her body was carved hollow, and within that space, there was distance enough for stars to swim.

"Impossible," she whispered like a last breath. She stared at the woman in black who waited there with the patience of a noontime shadow. "It doesn't . . ."

Alondra smiled a row of grinning *X*'s. "It does. Both you and she know it's true."

Cait tried to reach something she could hold onto. The weightless instant stretched out in the sound after her last syllable. There was an absence there, a vacuum with its own pull, and for a moment, Cait didn't know if she still slept, only that the sound of the voice was everything.

And it was all true. She knew. The queen knew.

The rush of knowledge slammed her with the force of a car crash, invisible but physical. Cait could feel the muscles in her head and neck clench, and realization rippled through her like she was water and it a stone.

"Tomorrow night, Cait MacReady." She lowered her hand, and her voice snapped back to normality. She stood and made ready to leave, pausing as if to feel the sunset on her skin, features impenetrable and revealing nothing. "Should we send a car to meet you?"

Cait struggled to form an answer. This conversation took place a world away somehow. "What? No." She sounded unconvincing even to herself. "How would you know where to find me?"

Alondra made a sound of disapproval, teeth white beneath the traces of black lipstick.

Another realization crept into place for Cait: No Tomorrows knew exactly where she lived and resisting them would be impossible, even if she'd wanted to. She was caught in the riptide of this, something too strong to stand against. She wanted to go along with them. They wanted something she had.

They wanted her. The realization was beautiful, but it twisted her insides around in the same moment.

"No, wait!" Cait sat up and tried to get out of the chair to follow, but her whole body moved slowly and with the pins and needles from being slept on. "You have to tell me!"

Alondra turned, and her smile wore pity like a mask. "You wouldn't believe it even if you understood. And the queen thinks that you need both." Her eyes flicked up and down Cait in an instant, and she couldn't even bother to sneer. "Do not disappoint her." Her noose braids swung as she turned away.

The silent man moved, panther quiet. Cait had all but forgotten he'd even been there. The tattoos on his arms spelled out entire languages that escaped her, though flashes of it were familiar: a scattering of symbols and sigils all but lost in the confusion of the whole. He stared at her and made a motion with his hands, fingers bending over themselves like morning glory vine on a derelict building. As quickly as it formed, they flexed into normality. He offered neither assurance nor explanation.

The sunset behind the two of them showed the whole of the world beyond the horizon burning.

Cait let it burn as her eyes closed, lids heavy as mountains.

༄

"Just relax, girl. Trace has got you."

"How long have you been there?" Cait's eyes opened to it being dead night outside, the salon now washed in hot pink from the neon sign.

"Long enough to know a couple things. Lay yourself back down, so we can get this done and dusted."

"This is all wrong. They knew about the book." She tried to sit up, and Trace held her down with a stony grip.

"No more dripping. Besides everyone knows about the Book. They leave it in hotels for free. Know a guy who's built a house with Gideons."

Cait couldn't even laugh. "I have to see Rico."

"Whatever trouble he's in, it can wait another while, so we can get this cleaned up. Boy should watch who he does business with."

"A mess since forever, right?"

"I know it."

Trace's fingers danced over the now-violet hair, shades darker than asked for. "Just hurry, please."

 formula

"Ya know that the rain makes the frogs come up here in a wave," Link said, his voice cigarette-rough but sweetened with a lilting, mid-Southern twang. "Streets would be slick with 'em all flooding up from the river."

They were rolling down Riverside Drive at a good clip, pacing the LA River as it surged from last night's downpour. It slapped against slanted concrete banks, blackly turbulent, choked with refuse washed from a thousand streets.

"I've heard." Cait could only make for hollow conversation. The nails on her first two fingers were bitten ragged. "But it rained last night, and I don't see a one."

"Maybe they know something you and I don't." He halfheartedly laughed and shoveled some shelled peanuts into his mouth. "Figure it's bad if it's enough to scare the little ribbits right out of Frogtown."

"Maybe." Cait let it hang. Normally she liked riding with Link. He was cheaper than a real cab, played better music too. But dread gnawed at her too much to enjoy the ride tonight. Not even Gene Vincent's "Bluejean Bop" settled things, rattling out of the ancient Cadillac's speakers.

"Remind me of the turn," Link said.

The light on his slicked hair made Cait think of the silent man with the knife. She swallowed hard. "Colhill, Link. End of the street. Closest to the river."

He swung it hard, turning past a bakery that somehow spewed smoke, lit yellow by the streetlights in the dusk. The end of the street got dark even before it hit the fence and the concrete slope of riverbed.

Link sized up the street, all watching eyes and sideburns. "Nice street. Looks like a lotta not asking questions about the neighbors."

The guitar track unreeled slow and easy, but the undercurrent in it sang of drives revealing themselves.

"Can you turn that off for a second, please?" she asked.

"Not Gene, nope." But the volume dropped down anyway.

"End of the street."

"You want I should wait for you?"

She tapped her fingers, skipping the raw tips of the bitten nails. "Go back up the block if you want, but I should be okay. Just trying to settle my nerves."

"At a look, that's going to take about a quart of bourbon."

Cait said nothing as she got out of the car and stepped to the curb. "There's a phone outside that bakery. I'll call when I need a lift back."

Link nodded and turned the music back up. "This side's gonna be dead tonight. And I got a gig over on Ivar in a couple hours. I gotta get handsome before that so don't be long."

"I won't be. Just gonna give Rico a piece of my mind."

"You always made a good pair."

She slammed the door with all her weight and said, "Things end all the time, Link." She leaned back through the window and passed him a ten. "That's to stay close by."

He took the bill and folded it twice before jamming it into a jeans pocket without shifting. "Like I'd leave the city limits. Seen the Central Valley, and I got no use for it."

The Caddy pulled away and made a loping U-turn in too tight a space, slow and graceful. As the taillights shrank, Cait wished he was staying, but she'd never have asked. Violet without depth or feature ate the sky above, not even the stars showing.

The place Rico rented had been built sometime after the last flood but looked like it had taken a beating anyway. The naked lemon tree in the yard showed only a couple shriveled fruit and leaves that seemed to cling out of sheer, thorny spite. Everything looked sick in the dingy porch light.

Something flickered on the other side of the drawn curtains, the faintest cast of blue to it. It moved creepy, like a ghost.

It's just the television. Get moving.

Cait took measured steps up to the porch and knocked on the door out of habit. It moved perceptibly under the first rap of her knuckles, not even latched. The door didn't creak as it slid open the width of a hand.

The sliver of dark widened, more flickering at the edge of it and now a whispering voice with words she couldn't make out.

"Hello?" she called out stupidly.

Far away, the river burbled, still rain driven. That was her only answer. Her eyes adjusted to the gloom, and she could sense a rhythm to the lights now. She pushed against the door until friction caught it and the whine of a dry hinge cut.

"Rico?" Her voice couldn't fill a coffee cup, much less a house.

She tried to recall the layout. Tiny entryway, tiny living room, tiny hallway, tiny kitchen. All of those *tinys* stretched out grotesquely now, a series of tunnels with the faintest of lights at the end of them. Her heart picked up as she crossed the threshold.

The voice on the television resolved itself now. She focused on it as an anchor, leading her through the house.

"Coming up next on KNBC—"

She walked through the entry way, smelling only the wood and the dingy carpet, unable to see anything between the weak streetlights and the television.

"A special sixty-minute episode of *Quest 4*—"

The kitchen lay at the back of the house, lit only by the bounced light from the TV, mercurial and unpredictable now.

Rico, what the hell are you playing at?

"—followed by *Riptide* at its regular time slot."

The screen dimmed to nothing for a moment, and Cait caught her own breath as the hallway went dark. She forced herself another step, almost expecting the world to just simply run out at the next.

"Tonight on *Quest 4*, a special episode. An enduring mystery." The announcer's spoke with a stentorian voice, firm but open to possibility. Cait knew the program but never watched it with intention.

Space aliens and the Bermuda Triangle and escaped Nazis from WWII. A weird mix of plainly untrue and just plausible enough to keep the rubes tuned in. Can't believe it's still running.

She chuckled to herself.

Watkiss knows his game. Wonder if he's still stiffing his research staff. God knows I should have been paid double at least.

"Seven scientists disappeared, an entire facility perhaps destroyed but not abandoned."

She crossed to the end of the hallway and touched the wall, taking comfort from the rippled texture at her fingertips: cold and slick with glossy paint that reflected the television glare like rain on asphalt.

"The Blackrock Incident, more than twenty years ago now. Conflicting stories of disaster, but was there discovery within this tragedy? Do the ghosts of the past still haunt the facility?"

Cait's eyes finally caught up with the darkness, and she could see clearly enough to make her way. The television's light drew her. The room felt cool and drafty, too open.

"*Quest 4* cameras have been allowed inside Blackrock. These images you see are new and real. Before now, the federal government and industry have kept photographers and investigators out."

The screen displayed a black and white image of a desert landscape with a cluster of blurry buildings at its center. The center building stood only partially, collapsed or altered, something more than mere abandonment and time. Both the sand and sky were a near-uniform shade of bleary gray, overexposed.

The room went dark again as the screen dissolved to a shattered window frame on a black backdrop. Glass hung with outlines suggestive of knives.

"What really happened on that night in 1962? Did the accident lead to a breakthrough that is as yet suppressed? Or was the official story all there is to tell?"

She broke away and looked toward the narrow French doors to the backyard, hanging open. Light from the television painted the limits of the room, but there could have been anything beyond them. She stepped closer to look out.

"Tonight, on *Quest 4*, the tragedy of Blackrock, mysteries and revelations."

The light of the television now behind her and no longer distracting, she looked out into the backyard, riddled with low spikes of dead Bermuda grass that might yet revive in the rain. But now they were a carpet of sallow, grey nails pointed at odd angles. The edge of the dim light caught something. Cait tried to focus on it but couldn't.

"Blackrock, New Mexico. Two hundred miles from Santa Fe. The US government in conjunction with Split Energies built a secret facility at the height of the Cold War."

Cait fumbled along the wall, stretching until she found the Bakelite switch for the lights and tripped it on her second attempt. An audible snap erupted like a pane of glass breaking, and light flooded the kitchen, sweeping away the pull of the television spilling out to the backyard.

"On October fifteenth, 1962, work began on Project Windowsill, the paperwork around which is still highly classified. Theories have swirled around this for years. Were there aliens? Were they experimenting in higher dimensions? Perhaps something more."

Cait wasn't looking at the television, instead out among the dead grass and rain-wet clay. Someone was sleeping out there, face up to the stars.

ᴄ૨ᴦ

She perched on the rickety chair for she didn't know how long. She couldn't recall ever having sat down.

Too tired. Too little sleep last night. Too much happening today.

"Scientists consulted by *Quest 4* are still at a loss to explain the apparent physical anomalies suggested by the Blackrock Anvil."

The television voice sounded more subdued now. Maybe she'd turned it down before realizing that it was Rico out there in the backyard and that he hadn't breathed the entire time she'd watched.

His breath hot and sweet on my neck as he lay kisses over my carotid like he could taste the rush of blood beneath.

She tuned out the TV. It was stupid now. It didn't matter. Nothing mattered, other than the fact that he wasn't sleeping. He was dead. Cait swallowed down the confirmed fear, and it tasted of yesterday's vomit.

Rico lay there, dressed and still. She had to see him and make sure. Maybe it was bullshit, and he was just drunk or even doped up despite his swearing himself clean. He did that sometimes, and even though they'd fought about it, he still did. One set of lies, Cait could take, but when those lies became the foundation?

The drawer came open, and she felt around for the candles and matches she knew were there. It only took three tries to find them, fingers sliding over junk and debris.

Between the candle, the TV, and the kitchen light, she could almost see clearly as she walked out. The grass crunched softly beneath her feet, steps deliberate and slow, though her heart rattled around her chest like a loose bone in a garbage disposal.

There was no blood, though she'd somehow expected that. Something glittered in the light, hard and metallic. She knelt down, drawn to it. As she got closer, she realized small scatterings of them clustered around points of his body, his hands and a halo around his head. Like a constellation of shell casings after a shooting.

Milagros.

Cait's fingers closed around the closest group, all linked together, from those around his head. She carefully looked not at him but at the small silver charm. It was an eye, open wide to see who knows what. The detail in it had almost been worn smooth with wear from handling and worrying. Cait recognized it. She'd held it before but only when part of the string of charms that Rico had carried in his pocket. She remembered feeling it the first time, still warm from his body heat as she held it in her palm.

It was well cold now.

She pocketed it and forced herself to look at him now. His closed eyes and placid face rested, receptive and somehow knowing as if having heard the secret of everything and satisfying all the curiosity he'd ever have.

Cait could still smell blood, even over the tang of her dye and the dry whisper scent of the dead grass and the still wet ground. It must have been there, but she couldn't find any.

His palms were turned up, and now that her eyes had adjusted, she realized that they'd been altered: the one closest to her cut widthwise with tiny curls at either end like lips teased into a smile.

"Oh God, Rico, what did they do to you?" she whispered. "You stupid kid." The tears were hotter than suicide blood as they ran down her face, but she didn't gasp or choke at the sensation.

She sucked a breath in, ragged, and looked at his face again. The eyes were closed, but they were wrong, as if sunken or maybe even melted away. Something marked the lower lids, a memory of makeup only partially washed off. She leaned closer and smelled the blood or whatever else the eyes had rested in. But they were gone.

She couldn't bring herself to flip the lids back to confirm it, but they were gone.

A helicopter roared somewhere in the distance, and the sound of the crickets rose up to meet it. Cait looked up to the sky and wondered what he might have seen last and who had done all this. The answer glared at her, obvious as a bullet dug out from an entry wound, nestled right up against the bone.

No Tomorrows had done this. They'd laid him out in some kind of pose of cosmic supplication, Rico giving himself up to the night and whatever was in it, palms turned upward to accept whatever gifts came.

Palms.

Cait pulled herself up and walked around his head to the dark side of his body. The candle burned strong, and the scattered milagros glinted warmly as the grass made brittle sighs beneath her feet.

She knelt down a second time and looked at the hand on the blind side, his left. There was a cut in it as in the other. But this one opened partially, invitingly. The smell of blood was stronger here, and she held herself against it. She looked closer at the wound, seeing it bulge strangely like a misshapen tumor beneath the skin.

The candlelight revealed there in the gash two brown eyes cast upward but far removed from their regular orbits. Cait knew that they were gazing up to the stars, but she felt the dead gaze boring down to her heart, which ceased its rattling and came to a stop as she dropped the candle.

The light reflected in Rico's brown eyes until the candle burned out.

$\sim$

"One more time," the detective said with patience of an iron statue. "From the beginning." He was black and heavyset and grandfatherly, but the kind of grandfather who gave out too much unsolicited advice and expected it to be accepted gladly. His name was Trager, that being the first word he'd said to Cait, followed by the phrase "Open Door" like that had weight.

She stared into the brown eyes behind the glasses. He'd slipped them up every time he needed to read her face. "I came to check on Rico. We'd had a fight the night before, and I worried." The words dragged out of her, a load of bricks carried one by one.

"Your boyfriend?" The dark brow furrowed. "He threatened to hurt himself?"

"No. I told you before." She wanted to sit down, but someone occupied every seat: LAPD uniforms or any of the coroner's crew not loitering by the white-sheeted body on the gurney in the backyard. In the daylight, it didn't look so bad. Not like that half-lit night, imagining more than there was.

His eyes were staring back.

"Ex-boyfriend. But we're still friendly."

"And you were dissatisfied with this." The question mark was left off.

Cait felt her fingers fidget and twist and willed them to stop. "Only sometimes. Look, this wasn't jealousy or a spurned lover thing. And he wasn't the type to kill himself."

"Nobody said that. But you did say you were worried."

She struggled for his name, lost in the fog between the call to the cops and the call to Link to tell him to get out of there and the flood of everything else in finding Rico's body and then formulating a story that would lead to the fewest number of questions. Even the relief that she wouldn't have to put up with his bullshit anymore and her shock at that relief.

Or that his bullshit had gotten him killed. Both those had to wait though.

"Officer . . ."

"Detective. Trager," he corrected. Then a smile. "I worked too hard for that to let it go easily, Ms. MacReady."

"I'm sorry."

"And there's the books. Almost like his own collection." Trager's eyes narrowed. "Was that a—"

"Hey, Jack, are we almost done here?" Another voice stabbed deep, cutting Trager off and coming from the sandy-haired and mustachioed second detective who'd dealt with the body and the coroner's crew. His voice was tight and short, clipped as his own motions that felt as impatient as an AA meeting about to break into a fistfight.

"A little courtesy here, Fellowes." Trager turned back to Cait and offered a smile. "My partner doesn't like getting up this early."

"You mean staying up this late."

"Same difference."

"I just want to know if I can go," Cait asked. "I was working all last night. Well, night before, and I'm about ready to fall over."

"I can see that." He glanced down to the clipboard and paperwork that had remained mostly unfilled during the interview. "We have enough to get our preliminary report done, but I have to ask you to come in again and make a full statement."

"Okay, yeah." She struggled to put a sentence together. "So I'll just go to the station on . . . San Fernando, right? That's the closest one."

The two cops looked at each other and chuckled without humor.

"Oh no," Trager answered. "You'll have to go all the way downtown."

Cait couldn't stop her face from scrunching up. "That's a trip. What dragged you out here for this?"

"Open Door," Fellowes said. He popped a cigarette into his mouth but left it unlit. It rolled from one side to the other. "What, you didn't know? I mean, come on, with the nature of the body and all." He drew X's over his eyes and pointed to his left hand, making a cutting motion.

"Knock it off. Not everyone keeps current," Trager growled. His left hand came up to an impatient point.

Thankfully, that tone hadn't come out for her. Cait watched Fellowes shrink from it like a slug from salt.

"Sorry, Jack. I mean, just, come on. This is a weird one. Even Miss Librarian here can see that." He offered a smile that wouldn't make it to the operating table.

Trager shook off the irritation and tried a grin of his own. It fit pretty well. "I'm sorry. My partner means to say that because of the nature of this case, it goes to Open Door. Which is us. And we work out of downtown. But not the fancy part."

"Only the best!" Fellowes added as he lit the cigarette, visibly relaxed.

"Open Door?" Cait asked. "So, what, 'weirdo squad'?"

"You could say that." The smile widened. "Maybe I underestimated you."

"You didn't." Cait wanted for a place to sit, but none of the chairs had been vacated. Nobody was in a hurry. "My mom's brother was a cop a long time ago, over in Venice mostly."

"Then you know all about weirdos."

"Yeah. That Skullface Killer still keeps me up at night."

"Well, our specialty is a very specific kind of weirdo. Multiple killers or those with definite, uh, overtones."

Cait made a funny face at that.

"He means 'occult,'" Fellowes interjected with puff of smoke as the exclamation point. "The religious, the cultish, the unexplained, and the plain goddamned scary."

"At least the press isn't here," Trager muttered. "You know, you're a credit to that badge."

Fellowes saluted cockeyed and took a drag that drew down a quarter of the Marlboro. "Can we go now? Paperwork calls, and we can't time that out on general."

"Keep your shirt on."

Cait sighed and felt a weight slipping off her. She'd managed to keep No Tomorrows out of this and the meeting at the salon and any mention of her business, even with Rico's books. She tried not to think about where they'd come from since he wasn't holding any for her.

This was just a weird, freak event that Rico had gotten himself into and Cait just happened to know him. Nothing more.

She couldn't answer whether fear drove her or something else. She didn't owe No Tomorrows anything and getting rid of them would be a positive.

But still, she didn't mention them.

Two cops against whatever the hell No Tomorrows really is? They can't keep people from killing one another, much less entire gangs. Better they keep their noses out.

"Yeah, just a minute."

"Come on, corned beef special at the academy this morning. We can still make it before the rush." Fellowes put his weight on one foot and then the other like a bored, hyper teenager.

"I thought smokers weren't food obsessed."

"I'm trying to quit."

"Try harder. Now just go wait in the car."

As if that had been a code phrase, the coroner's orderlies began to half lift, half roll the gurney out, and the kitchen vacated.

Cait fought with herself to keep from running to one of the chairs. "Okay, so I go downtown and ask for one of you?"

Trager snapped out a card, worn on the corners as if it had ridden around with him for a long time. "Only me. If I'm out, have them call me in. I'll take your statement."

"Trusting." She watched him from behind the card he held up as a talisman.

"I'm the senior officer, and this is just policy. I don't make it, but I do follow it." His face softened. "Are you okay? Do you need a ride back home or to a friend's? You probably shouldn't be alone."

Friends? Which friends. Vivian? That bridge burned a while back. Maybe Trace. Maybe Hypatia if she wasn't holed up with her weirdo friends again wheatpasting anarchist handbills on every telephone pole in sight.

There weren't many options. Friends weren't something that had come easily or quickly to Cait and never would.

"There isn't really anyone I could stay with. My folks are out in Riverside now, and I still have work to do."

"Just call in. Tell them you have a detective's excuse." He smiled again and slipped the glasses off, interview over.

Physical relief flooded her, and she didn't bother to correct him. Besides, the library was just a job. The book trade was her work. No. Not even that. The trade was just a way to get her real work out there. The codex was just the start. That was real. Everything else had been practice.

"We'll see. And thanks."

"Sure thing." He stood and didn't turn, though just the two of them remained.

"Anything else?" she asked with the last bits of her energy. If he pressed her, she'd have said just about anything in order to sit down.

"Just one question. What was it that you were concerned about? You said he wasn't the type to, you know, cut himself. But you were worried." The brow remained unfurrowed as if he already knew the answer but wanted to test her reply.

"Just that, well, he used to drink. And he did pills sometimes. Years ago. It's one of the things that broke us up."

"He couldn't choose?"

"Yeah."

"Well, for what it's worth, I don't think he did."

The thought sank into her like an anvil, but she didn't answer. She tried selling numbness for the next little while.

"We'll let you go for now, but come in no later than the day after tomorrow to swear out a statement. If there's anything else you want to add to the investigation, call me immediately." He sighed. "My partner is short-tempered and rude but sometimes correct. We get the odd cases, and any help we can get in solving them is always appreciated, no matter how strange the help is. You understand?"

"I don't. Like those bullshit psychics?"

"Wrong kind of bullshit. Never had a case solved by an astrologer. Have cleared some with aid from institutionalized patients who only spoke nonsense, though, but nonsense that applied to us. And there was the one where the break came from that damn TV show. I can never remember the name. Think it's still going."

"This doesn't sound like police work," Cait suggested. "Not like my uncle talked about."

"I've learned that sometimes cops don't know that much about police work, 'specially today." Trager sighed, a flash downpour of exhaustion. "It's sure not what I set out to do, but sometimes the job calls you, not vice versa."

"Now *that* I get."

"Keep the card. We'll talk soon."

He strode over the dead lawn and disappeared into the house. Cait followed after he'd left and slumped down into the wicker-backed chair in the yellow kitchen and stopped holding everything back. She stayed for more than an hour as it all flowed out of her.

☙

Cait awoke in her loft, dimly remembering the ride back and calling off her next couple shifts and the gruff reply from her boss asking for a written excuse from an actual detective when she came back. If she was coming back. She waited for a reaction from the threat, but it never came.

The sun slid toward afternoon through the tattered lace curtains over the kitchen window. She'd had them ever since she left home, sewn by her and her mother over an afternoon with a brushfire in the distance. The pattern was unique, made more so by age and imperfection. Light poured through the webbed fabric, projecting its fingerprint.

Without thought, she turned the switch to play the record on the turntable, and the dry, skittering drums of "Heart and Soul" by Joy Division started up. The music rolled past her, echoing around the empty space of the apartment, making it feel vast.

She checked the paper aging on the slanted boards by habit, ran it under her fingers, searching for the desired crispness, not finding it yet.

The routine settled her, even if the results were lacking. Until she remembered the silent man and Alondra with her twin nooses tied in glossy black. Or maybe she'd dreamed that too. The day before was a blender, full of sensation ground down to a vaguely numb pulp with just flashes of memory whipping past her but too quick to be caught. But those stuck or at least in passing cut her enough to be remembered.

She rotated the jars of perfumes steeping on the shelf, handfuls of crushed flowers swirled into rectified spirits. The petals themselves drained to just ghosts, all but leeched of color. A deep breath of the 190-proof liquor was enough to get her light-headed. The Russian guy she bought the spirits from could drink half a bottle before falling over, a real role model. Lavender, rose, coriander, lily, she counted off the jars, shaking them to check the legs and make sure the seals still held. Too much moisture would muddy the scent.

The blacking lamp with its multiple wicks needed fuel. She burned animal fat mixed with kerosene to maximize sootiness for aging. The four wicks sagged, left long, looking like bent and blackened pinkie fingers jutting out of the corners of the copper lamp. The top of it showed a patina of oily smudging from hundreds of hours of use.

No thought as she turned and pulled the jar of clarified yak butter from the small refrigerator and the small tin of kerosene from the cabinet under the sink. No thought, only the mechanical action of warming a half-cup of fat in the skillet, rendering it liquid enough to prime the works.

She didn't think about the two eyes tucked into Rico's hand. She dwelled upon it, unshakably. It was that or think about the hands on the frontispiece of the *Smoking Codex* and how one of them smiled and one of them saw with its own unblinking eye buried in the palm. That image took up a home in her head until she smelled the butter burning on the stove.

Without thought, she grabbed for the handle and was jolted by the iron's heat. It shot up her arm, making her drop the pan back to the burner by reflex. She swore wordlessly, just a cry of pain.

It focused her, shaking everything else away.

She snapped the burner off, opened the window over the sink, and ran cold water into a bowl lying there, shoving ice into that. She held her hand there until the pain shut off and a little longer for good measure.

The first thought that came to her was a question she couldn't answer. The same from this morning. Why hold back on No Tomorrows? These cops had to know them, maybe even suspected them already. And if they were responsible for Rico's death, saying nothing was . . .

She couldn't find the right word for it. Wrong? Self-preservation? Cowardice? There're people one just doesn't cross.

Or do business with. So I just cancel the meeting. Call them up and say it's off. Only they won't take no for an answer.

Only they may already know how to find me here. They found me at Distress easy enough. No running from this.

The street outside the window was sketched out in crazy shadow. Everything was turning sideways in her head as she peered into the shadows for people watching the place and laughed at herself.

Whatever the fuck. They already know me, and they want what I have. Even if what I have shouldn't exist, even if they shouldn't know about it.

And that bit at her more than anything else, more than the misplaced eyes, more than the straight razor that hung on the silent man's hip.

She wrapped the pan's iron handle with a towel and poured the scorched butter into the fuel well of the lamp. The room smelled of burnt fat. The welt on her palm began to throb, even wrapped with ice. She just focused on that. That much was real.

The phone rang three times before she noticed it. The last call she'd gotten was from Rico, and that hung on her before she moved to pick it up.

"Yeah."

"Cait? Praise Jesus." Valerie's cigarette-ruined voice creaked out of the other end. "You're hard to find."

"Not hard enough," she sighed. "Val? Is that honestly you?"

"Yeah, I'm surprised too. Don't give me a reason to hang up."

"I won't." Cait drew a breath and felt her ribs tighten. "I was just thinking about you this morning."

"That you'll apologize and go legit?"

"Neither of those is likely."

"Too bad. And it's too bad I can't ever sell anything you bring me. I don't traffic in books I can't certify."

"You're still worried about answering the wrong questions. Why are you calling?" She walked across the room with the handset in her fist, coiled cord stretched out, and turning down the music.

A distant, wracking cough erupted before the reply, "I got those copies of the *Papier Gemini* you were asking after a little while back. Weird-smelling guy from Azusa. Didn't know what he had. I'll make you a deal."

"Two months ago, this would have mattered."

"I can't turn back time. You want 'em or not?"

Cait tried to piece together what she'd even wanted them for. Some client. Something. But it didn't come to her. That happened before yesterday, so the meaning was lost. It simply didn't apply anymore.

"Cait? You there?" The concern in the voice stretched thin.

"Uhm, yeah. Sorry." The burn on her hand throbbed, red paint splattering behind her eyeballs. "Yeah, I don't think I can use those unless you wanted to let them go cheap."

"I didn't get where I am by giving money away."

"Your reputation remains unspoiled. Are we done here?"

The line held, Valerie breathing at the edges of the call. It wasn't her regular shortness of breath but something else. Both of them had been dancing around it.

"Are you okay?"

"I already answered that," Cait snapped. "Or have the hormone treatments eaten your brain?"

"That would have hurt. From a friend."

Cait didn't have an easy reply. Her pulse thundered, and her stomach soured.

Valerie took a deep breath and let it out cold. "Look, just 'cause I wasn't born a woman doesn't mean I can't be a cast iron bitch. So keep it up."

The shock snapped the pain away for a moment. "Jesus. Jesus, I'm sorry, Val. I didn't . . ." Cait's voice trailed off, lost.

"Didn't you?"

"No. I just. Shit." She put her back to the wall and slumped down under a terrible weight. Her breath sucked in and came out a dry sob. "Rico's dead, Val. He's dead, and someone did stuff to his body, and I think they want me too."

"Aw, kid. I knew he was in trouble, but he didn't tell me how bad."

"Wait. You *talked* to him?"

"Yesterday. He was waiting for me to open."

"But he . . . I mean, he wasn't working for you."

"Grow up, Cait. He worked for anyone who could help him make his rent. He just didn't want you to know about me."

Cait flashed on the books in Rico's house, and it made a lot more sense now. They were for Valerie. And Cait's wares weren't welcome any longer. Valerie's requirements for actual provenance and authenticity kept her and Cait on the outs. And once out with Valerie, it was as if you'd always been out.

"Jesus fuck." The sob was gone, replaced by a swarming of emotion. "Well you aren't the only one he's been doing business with. You heard of No Tomorrows?"

"Only what I see in the *Times* over scrambled eggs and Bloody Marys, which isn't much. And I don't pay attention to the crime pages."

"They're all crime pages. Rico set something up with them. I think. I think it's what got him killed."

"What is it? And why you?"

"They seem to want a book of mine."

"Not discriminating customers, I see."

"Ha." Cait's laugh was weak. "That's where you're wrong. They don't want a copy. They want an *original*."

"I don't understand."

"You're only interested in history, forget it." She shifted the phone to the other side, arm across her body. "They found Rico and used him to find me. They want a book I wrote."

"I still don't understand, but it's early yet. Look, he left me an envelope to give you. One of those padded jobs. I shake it, and it rattles inside."

Cait sat up slowly. "Well don't break the thing!"

"It's not fragile. I think it's a cassette." The snap of a lighter popped like flinty static, followed by a sizzle and a deep inhale made smooth with smoke. "He told me to call you about it around now. Couple hours ago, honestly, but I've been busy at my *therapy*. It's that time of year, you understand."

"I said I was sorry."

"I heard you, but you've earned a little spite."

"How was he?" Cait asked. He'd been evasive on the phone with her, defiant and even abusive. But that wasn't all him. She'd pitched things up all on her own. Without realizing it, her free hand had twisted up in the loosely coiled plastic cord. She pulled at it gingerly, dodging the spikes of pain.

"He was Rico, kid. Only more so. Cagey. Didn't even ask me about the hundred I owed him from the track. Lousy *Quartz City* in the fifth."

"Focus." Cait winced at the stab of pain from the cord slipping over her palm.

The cigarette breathed through the phone for Val. "He was scared, Cait, worried that you wouldn't get this whatever it is. And it was weird. He met me at my car and—"

"He knew where you lived?"

"Settle down. He's not my type."

"Yeah, okay."

"It was like he'd been waiting for me, didn't want to meet me at the shop. Came out of nowhere, looking over his shoulder. Hollow eyes, no sleep."

"Was he on anything?"

"If he was, I don't want any of it. Just looked like anxiety. But that's like the smog here, fact of life."

"Did he say anything else? About me or whatever?"

The cough came out like a bunch of celery being ripped. "Just that he'd, well . . . that he'd screwed up. He said it was in here." There was a small rattling, broken toy sounding.

"Was he being followed?" Cait thought of the street outside but didn't step to the window this time.

"Not that he said. But he didn't stay on any one foot for too long. Dropped the envelope and took off."

"When was this?"

"Oh, about the time I went down to open. Maybe close to noon."

"And you didn't call me then?"

"Cait. Sweetheart. You're lucky I'm calling you at all. I thought about throwing this in the trash, but Rico was dependable enough. And if you're saying he's dead . . ."

"Saying just that."

"Then both you and I owe him more than he's gotten so far. Maybe there's something on this that'll help."

"I'm . . . dammit. I'm really sorry, Val. About the crack and everything else."

"Apology accepted, but if you don't buy this *Gemini* volume from me for a good price, we're through."

"I don't want to be through."

"I'll be here until seven. Got an estate dump to sift through."

"There's gold in those obituaries."

"Yeah, most of it the fool's variety."

Cait hung up the phone with a clatter. She pulled back the yellowed curtain and watched the street. The light slanted harder now, making constructivist shapes of the shadows, overlaid by the organic curling of the lace. Nothing seemed more sinister or wrong than before, but a thought kept gnawing at her, that someone watched her just as they had Rico. That he led them to her.

A more frightening thought, they already knew her, and he had merely gotten in the way.

QUEEN OF NO TOMORROWS

She watched a white van, its sides laced in mud or rust, as it crawled down the mostly empty street. Kids walked past with faded, neon shirts peeking out from open ratty jackets. Marvin the homeless dude sat next to the trash can staring into the corner phone; homeless maybe, but he had a permanent address there. Everything was usual. Regular. Normal.

But nothing was. Rico was dead, and Cait now had a date with his ghost. She placed a call to Link and got ready while she kept an ear open for his return call.

༄

The envelope smelled like flop sweat as she opened it up in the back seat of Link's Cadillac. It was 8:15, and the night settled over the basin. City lights bounced off the bottoms of clouds, making everything seem trapped under a great lid.

"Back home?" he asked as the car started up.

"No time for that." Cait shoved her good hand into the bag and came out with a sixty-minute cassette, no case. Written in capital letters too big for the label were the words "FOR CAIT."

"I need you to play this. You got a deck in here, right?"

"Yep. Not like you can play records in a car. Well, you can, but it's a lot less fun than it sounds like." He took the tape between his first two fingers, curled as if around a smoke. "Hits picked to click?"

"Raves from the grave," Cait replied. She sat up so straight that her back never touched the seat, pulled as tight as possible without shattering. "Turn that up." The cold air rode over her exposed back, making gooseflesh on her arms.

Only an empty hiss came from the tape. It loomed with phantom sibilance over the rumble of the engine.

"Where are we going?" Link asked again. "You want a mind reader, you call my sister. She'll say anything you want."

"Cherokee. The Last Prayer Club."

"Funny. You don't look stupid. 'Specially not in that dress."

Cait wasn't dressed for royalty, but she could receive a queen at least. She wore a neat, black dress with a silhouette that promised nothing but business and severity. She hoped it would be enough to shore up the feeling of having been hollowed out and scraped clean by the last day or so.

"Why aren't I hearing anything?" She tried not to panic but felt her fingers digging into the beaten, vinyl back seat. She could only hear herself breathing, and it sounded like a bomb ready to go off.

A click and a rattle. "It wasn't rewound. Unkind." Another metallic sound of insertion and a whine of motors. "Give it a second."

Thunk.

The car pulled away from the curb with a shrug of power from the V-8 and the peel of whitewalls off asphalt.

Cait waited to hear something.

"Hey, Roja. I sure hope you get this. You and Val get along like my aunts, but they always wise up and know they're family in the end." Rico's voice was weary, just like he'd gotten off the phone with her the morning before.

"It's all shit right now, and maybe you won't even listen to this 'cause you love being right and all that."

The lights along Los Feliz Boulevard were all polite and low, genteel old houses on the edge of what passed for the commercial district before things spilled out into Hollyweird and went into the slurry of advertising and empty pop culture enterprise and old money that was the Westside. Cait stared at the shapes of Mission- and Craftsman-style homes, which were now worth what small cities had cost in the time of their building.

"And you're going to love this, but you were right. I shouldn't have done this. I'm a quick learner like that. Sometimes you're fast enough to catch the snake without getting bitten. Thought I was. Really did." He sounded drawn out now. "But you gotta believe me when I tell you that I didn't bring them to you. These No Tomorrows cats? They got their own pull."

Cait wanted to punch through the window next to her but drew that fury in like medicine.

"I met Ariela. You're gonna know her. I met her, and it was like she'd seen this all before. She knew who you were. She talked about our meeting like it was your book, like you made it. Crazy, right? It's just another copy like all the others, just mystic garbage.

"They were talking to me because they knew you'd just run if they came past me to you. God, they know stuff. How do they know it?"

Rico shifted, making a muffled sort of snake-sliding noise, and sighed.

"You know, when I was a kid, like yesterday, I thought there wasn't anything I wouldn't do for twenty-five large. I had a price. And now I think about it, I was wrong. I was wrong, and I couldn't talk to you then because nobody fucking could, Roja."

She didn't cry, but her anger burned terribly. It made the searing of the welt on her hand feel like the merest trickle of the river in the middle of summer. This was a winter flood, scouring concrete banks and turning over bodies thought long buried.

"God, I've been clean for months now. I couldn't tell you that either. There'd be no end to it. And I got this money, and I swear I could buy a hill of dope, buy forever in dope for me. And I can't even do that."

Cait ate at herself now, fingernails pressed into her opposite arms, leaving tiny crescents behind.

"And maybe this is too late, but I'm sorry everything went like everything did. Pride's a bitch. So's fear. And when you're shown that maybe everything's already happened, and it doesn't matter so just roll with it and profit? I'm afraid I did.

"But maybe it ain't too late," Rico's ghost said as the tape warbled, or maybe it was his own raw breakdown. "If something happens, you gotta know it was them. That guy Tácito. That means 'quiet,' I guess. It's him. He's stone cold like all the cholos could only ever pretend to be. God, he's real."

"Goddammit, Rico, you idiot," Cait said like it mattered still.

"You can tell the cops, but what's another street hustler, right? Just a little fish got eaten by a shark. No big." Something that sounded like a breath of futility echoed through the speakers now. "But if I'm right, whatever they want from you, they want 'cause it's got power for them. Bruja Halloween stuff. You can see it in their gestures and the way they talk. It's all a ceremony to them. Everything's a ceremony.

"Even me."

She refused to cry but instead burned on the inside. The traffic lights glowed Christmas red and green.

"Goodbye, Cait. Goodbye, girl."

A distant click sounded and a ratcheting sound and then the hiss she'd heard before.

"I'm going to just roll, uhm, some Blasters now. You good with that?" Link's dark eyes watched with sympathy in the rear view, but his hands only left the wheel to pop the tape and switch a new one in. He offered back the old one, and she hesitated before taking it and shoving it back in the bag, throwing that to the floorboards.

She nodded and did nothing more.

"You still want to go to the Last Prayer?"

"More than ever."

Rapid-fire guitar and piano ripped from the speakers as they drove through Hollywood.

A hundred different shades of black loitered in front of the club. Glossy vinyl jackets, denim straps and shrouds, rubber with a flat sheen formed a patchwork second skin on some. Club-goers smoked and laughed, metal rings in their ears and noses and faces all flashed like butterfly wings in flight. None of them watched as the Cadillac, tailfins and atomic-red brake lights and all, pulled up to the curb.

"Last chance," Link said over the idling engine. Beer barrel piano and shuffling beat with lyrics about sweat on a summer night all interplayed but couldn't lighten things.

"Wrong name." Cait checked her makeup in her pocket mirror. The lipstick went on too heavy, but that would be subtlety in this crowd.

"I know what I said."

"It's okay. I'm a guest tonight. Royal box and everything."

"Last time anyone offered me a 'royal box,' it was nothing like they'd sold it on."

Cait shot out a quick and quiet laugh. "You're a poet, Link."

"Only when the guitar talks." His face went stern and a little sad. "You know I ain't waiting out front for you, right? And I sure as hell won't go in there. That ain't rock and roll."

The beat pulsed out of the place like an inexorable machine, obliterating anything standing in its path. Even through the closed door of the car, it was persistent and penetrating.

"And that's what the first guys who heard the Stooges thought."

"Yeah, I guess." He turned from the rearview to see Cait directly. "You stay safe."

Cait popped the door open to the assault, heaving on the fourths and teeth-rattling cymbal smashes between.

"I think we're well past safe. Thanks." She handed him bills that he didn't count and instead folded neatly.

Two women in braided, black mohawks and horizontally streaked, bruise-blue and white warpaint watched Cait get out. The one on the left looked her up and down with eyes filled overfull with scorn.

"That's a nice silhouette, Violet," one of them said, lips black and pursed.

"But it's not getting you through the door," the other finished. Her smile made Cait want to slap it right off her face.

She took a step forward. "I'm here to see the queen, and if you don't want your paint mussed up, you better let her know." This wasn't the same insouciant defiance that used to work when she was sixteen and sneaking into bars past bouncers who buffaloed easy or just wanted to talk to a pretty girl a minute. The ice in her voice surprised even herself. These two useless doorstops were not standing between her and finding out why Rico was dead.

The two breathed seemingly in unison.

"That's cold," said the white-lipped one.

"Let her find her own reward then," the other answered with coal.

They parted, each pointing inward with the opposite arm, like a strangely flawed mirror.

For all the shadow outside, the interior of the club blinded her, casting everything in light so white that the edges burned blue or pink or purple. Cait's eyes couldn't adjust quickly enough to the glare from so much PVC and tarnished chrome. The hammering, droning beat of the music rattled the fillings in her teeth and make her eyeballs hurt. She'd been to countless shows and never felt anything like this. The crowd rode the beat right to a pulp.

No eyes spared her or the pair of guards any attention as they flowed through the club. Everyone stayed lost in the storm of sound that made glasses half full of liquor jump. Either that or they pranced and preened, there to be seen.

Cait saw freaks like she'd never really seen before. This was weirdness on an industrial scale. Half-shaved heads and piercings placed only for maximum shock value, bondage gear with the metal fittings worn down from use, and leather frayed and scarred into coarse suede. This was not an act of love but a mission to see if something could be bent before breaking. The crowd sought to make a point about how far they could go and still be human, all caught in incomplete transformation to something organic yet regimented and mechanical, joining a great machine that most people didn't even know existed.

The smells hammered Cait as hard as the sound. Alcohol, but for sterilizing and stripping. Sweat, human and tangy. Oil, a sheen on leather and skin. Bleach, searing. Smoke, cigarettes and cannabis tangled like ivy in the air. Perfume and crackling electricity, invisible and potent.

Dizzy in the tornado of input, she had nothing to hold onto, nothing but finding the queen and asking her.

Asking her.

Asking her what? What was it?

Something about Rico. Something about the book.

She blinked against a sudden strobe, the space behind her eyelids an endless seething of welted pink with afterimages blown out to meaninglessness. Only the echo of the terrible world that surrounded her remained. There was no safe place to hide.

Stumbling on something unseen, she caught herself and opened her eyes. Behind her, one of the twin mohawks said, "You wanted her, and now she is yours."

She didn't think about how she could hear them over the din.

In a corner of the club, somehow dark and shaded, protected from the searing blasts of klieg lights, sat a high, padded booth of unmarred red suede, rich with texture and variation. It looked just built, and maybe it was, night after night for the queen's pleasure.

Alondra saw Cait first, a look of muted surprise behind her dark glasses. Her lips pursed in surprise, though they were not marked with *X*'s as before, just black with what looked like stalactites at the corners, a permanent frown. She raised her left hand.

"So you came," she said.

"Alone." She wanted to wrap her arms around herself, but that would give too much away. "Though I have instructions for a friend to contact the police if I don't make it back from this meeting."

Alondra's eyebrow rose before she stifled a laugh. "¿Oh, la policía? Well that makes all the difference." She dropped her hand and turned to the man named Tácito and laughed again.

He smiled, mouthed a word, and made the sign of the *X* over his eyes and his left palm. Cait struggled to remember where she'd seen that before. The noise and smoke and lights pushed all other thoughts out.

Alondra turned back, stern. "Thank you for warning us, Cait."

The queen kept her back to the conversation, refusing to turn. She existed above it still and always would. Nothing here was yet worth her notice.

Alondra's voice cut through a break in songs. "Allow me to present to you my sister, Ariela Ramona Califia Gutiérrez, Nuestra Reina de Sombra y Silencio, the Queen of No Tomorrows."

The queen stood before the table and leather benches, braced by her sister and Tácito. As Cait's eyes adjusted to the unexpected dark, Ariela turned to face her. The queen was a woman lost to time. If these two women were sisters, Cait had to work hard to see it. Where Alondra was brown skinned, the queen was pale and delicate, not sickly but brittle. Ariela's face appeared more delicate and childlike, powdered pale as a doll. At least what Cait could see.

Ariela hid everything below her clear, blue eyes behind a veil, layers of clinging, diaphanous lace, though her jawline remained visible beneath it. Her dress was twenty shades of black, tight as a shroud to her waist but flowing from her hips like oil pooling in the tide. Cut beads of black glass were sewn along every hemline, tinier than an infant's fingernails, and the light danced across them. The dress itself didn't rustle or crinkle as she waited to be appreciated.

A light lace panel, transparent as a dying man's breath, spanned from her cleavage to her neckline. The shimmering fabric was bordered off by a choker of raw obsidian beads that looked sharp enough to cut at a distance. Beneath the lace, Cait glimpsed the outline of a tattoo: a whirlpool but more organic.

Datura.

It grew all over Los Angeles and Southern California, and its leaves were infused with potent alkaloids, enough to stupefy cattle, much less humans who handled it. Even the honey made from the flower could put some people under. Plenty of amateur mystics tried making it into tea or smoking the leaves and only earned trips to the emergency room or weeklong nightmares for their trouble.

Ariela brought the admiration to a close. She snapped open a fan and held it before her veiled face. Eyes the same color as her dress peered at Cait with expectation.

Cait could barely make out a dry whisper, and Alondra nodded.

"The queen is both disappointed that such a meeting had to be arranged and pleased that it is finally taking place." Alondra's hands rested at her sides now, fingers spread gently.

"Your majesty," Cait said to Alondra.

"Address her."

The queen's veil shifted as she smiled, and her dark-lined eyes crinkled in regard.

"Why do you want to see me?" Cait felt herself trying to remember her drama classes, where to speak from, anything to project with a little more authority. It all came out in a jumble of mismatched cues and stances.

"The queen knows," Alondra said, and Cait's eyes went back to her. "For the last time, address the queen. I am not important." There was strain in the last phrase but sugared heavily.

Cait sucked in a breath and steadied herself. "I'm sorry." She wondered if Tácito still played with his knives out of her view.

"The queen knows," Alondra continued, "that you are a seller of rare and unusual books." Something in her voice registered as *extra*, as it had back at the salon. It had fingers in it, fingers that worked Cait's ears and the brain between them. She could feel something in the words.

"There are lots of them in Los Angeles. Why me?" her eyes rested on the queen. "I'm no more or less special than any other."

A lie. There were plenty other book dealers. Vivian and Powers and Kent. That was just on the LA side of the San Gabriels. But not many did book restorations, offering only to sell the genuine article as it lay. None were forgers, or they'd managed to keep those parts of their business apart. No. All these people treated books like they were a monastic pursuit. Forgery was the ultimate sin, Vivian would always eagerly remind her.

"Maybe." Alondra's voice carried through the room with just a tickle on the last sibilance. "Maybe she sees something in you that is not in the others." Something that Alondra herself clearly did not.

Cait swallowed hard and wondered how No Tomorrows could possibly have found out. Not even Rico knew where Cait's books came from, just that Cait could get them and they were for sale. It was inconceivable.

But that didn't stop her palms from going damp with cold sweat.

"How can I help?" That wasn't the question she wanted to ask, but it was what came out. She felt heavy and lulled.

The queen and Alondra glanced at one another and nodded slightly. The queen whispered again. Cait thought she could almost understand it, but it slipped away.

Alondra removed her sunglasses and let out a long breath. Her eyes were dark in the bar's gloom, lit with impatience. "*Help*. Yes. What a perfect word." Her eyes were as dark as Rico's. "We're looking for a book. One that the queen is convinced only you can find for us."

"Maybe. But this takes some time." Cait spoke in controlled breaths, trying not to shake. Alondra's voice was grasping and penetrating.

"We have obligations that make time of the essence."

There was an urgency beneath her words, squeezed out from desperation and yielding diamonds, hard and sharp.

The queen was a believer, but Alondra was afraid of something.

That was a risk in the world of antique books, even more so when the occult and forbidden was a declared specialty. Just because Cait was clear in not believing a single word printed or promise made by these books, that didn't mean buyers didn't end up believing in her wares. Each of them was hungry for something, whether the volume was authentic or a forgery. Whether the book was written in the Enochian tongue or the confessions of the first hanged man or even the secret language of the Serpents on the Sand, all of them promised power.

And believers only ever wanted that.

"The *Smoking Codex*," Cait said gravely, unbelieving.

"Do you have it?"

The queen turned back to watch Cait, eyes narrowed now.

Cait's stomach boiled.

It's a book that doesn't exist.

It's a book I wrote.

She couldn't make the contradiction resolve itself, like pushing oil into a specific shape with only her bare hands. A glance at the ice-blue eyes told her that the queen would wait for an answer, but she would only accept one and no other.

The warring realities tangled in her head, each cutting the other with razors of certainty, flowing around the opponent's strikes. The heat of it made Cait sweat through her clothing. She could feel the bloom of perspiration across the low back of her dress, and even that didn't feel real.

The music cut out as surely as if the players had been murdered to no applause.

Cait coughed the dry patch out of her throat. "A singular volume."

The queen's pale-almost-translucent face didn't change, didn't smile or frown, only threw a glance at Alondra, and in that look, she asked for patience. Alondra nodded, but her mouth was pulled tight.

"You *know* it, or you *have* it?" she asked.

"Know it. Perhaps Mister Soame would—"

"And now for your painful pleasures!" shouted the announcer so loud that he must have been spitting blood. "Dreamless is on the stage!"

Alondra's face went bitter with a private disappointment. "Yes. Your employer. We would ask him if we could reach him and not a *recording*." Her fingers tightened and then flexed in unison, black nails shining over darker denim, simmering and impatient. Each of them was painted with a different symbol in white strokes the width of several hairs.

"He doesn't take calls directly. He's a man who values his privacy."

Even Cait couldn't believe her own lie. The thought of Rico breaking through the surface of a black sea and reaching out to her flashed across her mind and was submerged as quickly as it had come. There came another thought, and like a pair of eyes opening in a lacerated palm, the thought bored into her with a physical jolt. Electricity from the club melted any resistance she had, electricity from the tech-beat, electricity from the lights, electricity between the people dancing and pouring energy out of themselves until there was nothing left to give to the body music.

The music resolved itself into audible words for the first time since entering the club, and Cait couldn't bear to repeat them, but she heard them.

ROCK ROCK XXX-XXXX ROCK came the intonation from the band, but the two syllables were a mystery to Cait, only half heard. Whatever it was, the crowd knew their fullness and responded, thrusting against the cage around the performers and the tables in front of them until the whole place shook.

All sound left her, even the ringing of her ears.

"I wrote the codex. It's mine," Cait could hear herself saying. The words echoed as if spoken in a breathless cathedral, adherents waiting to hear and receive.

The queen's fan snapped shut like a finger bone breaking. She raised her hand as her sister had done, obscuring her already veiled lips.

"You are ready. We can speak." Her voice was unique, firm but wrapped in surprising warmth. Cait heard the voice clearly, down to the faint sibilance that might be called a lisp were it any stronger. The queen's words were sourceless, almost as if they'd come from behind herself. The whisper filled the room, every surface hummed from it. She shivered at the sound of it, arms crawling with it, cold even in the close and sweaty heat of the club.

"I'm so very glad," the queen said. "We can dispense with ceremony now." She stepped forward, seemingly without walking, and gently took Cait by the arm. Her fingers were neither warm nor cool. "Come with me."

Cait did as she was told, incapable of anything else.

"Subriemos," the queen whispered to Alondra.

"¿Estas seguro?" There was a flash of concern tempered by surprise on her face as she drifted back half a step to allow Ariela through.

The queen, slighter and shorter than Cait, looked her up and down once and turned back. "No tengo nada que temer de ella." There was a singsong note to her voice, something that picked at Cait. There was teasing as if they didn't expect her to understand the Spanish spoken between them. She knew enough that they believed she was no threat, that the queen had nothing to fear from her.

The beat continued, pulverizing everything around them and reshaping it to its own ends. None in the club fought it or even thought about it. They only loved it.

☙

The room above the club was spare and organic, rough-hewn. Slats of bare and ragged wood showed through crumbling plaster. The floor gave in places, nails sticking up just enough to be felt through the soles of her shoes, the irregularity comforting to her.

There was a dirty window, specks of grime like dead stars scattered against the dim yellow-green smear of light from Hollywood just outside. The light was trapped by dirty lace curtains cut in intricate shapes. In the center of the room lay a table and two chairs set to opposite sides. There was no adornment, no ornament. It was the plainest place in the world. Not even a pauper's tablecloth to cover anything.

"Please sit," said the queen. "I will take the farthest chair." Every word came with the slightest gesture, none of which was unimportant, all having weight that perhaps only Ariela herself understood.

Cait sat, and there was no comfort there. She still felt like her insides had been left out on the freeway and run over by a thousand pairs of wheels. She wondered why she couldn't hear the club anymore, beat banished and only the feeling that the world was very far away now even though the door was right there.

Alondra and Tácito stepped to the threshold, but the queen held up a hand to stop them. The pair watched her with suspicion but ultimately yielded. They melted back into the heated chaos that lay beyond the door. The only sound left was that of Cait shifting in her chair as she sat.

"What do you really want?" she asked.

"That is the question. And that's what gives you power, Cait." The queen drew a deep breath and the datura tattoo swelled between her breasts.

"I don't understand. This place is all unreal. I shouldn't be here."

"Where else is there to be? Back at your home? Running away? There is nowhere else. There is only right here. This place." The veil didn't move with her breath.

"Hollywood."

"If that's what you believe, I won't try to change your mind." Her smile was a shrug. "Just listen for a moment."

"I'm not going anywhere."

The queen's eyes closed in concentration, and Cait didn't mirror the gesture. "Listen." Ariela's voice swelled. "Think of time and that we are handicapped by it, believing that it has only one direction or that it moves at all."

"Spare me the physics lecture. Unless you like the sound of your own voice."

The queen's face flushed for a moment but went placid once more. "Belief is something that goes away when you stop believing. You can choose not to believe in gravity. And if you really feel that, I will take you to the roof and push you off myself. It won't matter."

"So much for my safety."

"Don't be a child, Cait. Your importance in this is something that you can scarcely comprehend. And that is because I have asked you here." Her fingers steepled and bent against one another, sheathed in sliced lace gloves.

"You have it backwards, right?" Cait scraped the chair across the uneven floor and sat up straighter. "You think I'm important, so *then* you find me and order me here."

"Invite," she said as if that distinction was more important than anything. "You could have refused. But you wouldn't."

"You would have forced me here. Or killed me like Rico." The statement stumbled out of her, unintended despite her searching for the words all night.

The queen's face softened for a moment, but her black eyes remained hard. "If your friend Rico is dead, that was not of my making. I wouldn't order such a thing."

"You'll excuse me if I don't believe you, your majesty. He was killed, and it was done with ceremony." She let the last word stab. Instead of looking at her teacher, she stared at the surface of the desk, trying to conjure detail from it.

"And we are not the only ones with manners in this city. Perhaps you should ask them." She shifted, bending and softening only a little. "But you wouldn't survive it, even if you were to find them.

"The death of your friend Rico was without con*sequence*."

Cait tried not to dwell on the meaning of the syllables being stretched. She was sure it meant something to the queen and her backward logic. "Tell him that. He has a better chance of believing you."

"That is outside my power. Perhaps."

Cait's eyes widened in disbelief, and she slapped a hand on the table. "You're telling me you can run around in time."

Her black eyes lit with recognition beneath perfectly drawn eyebrows. "No. But we are not so hobbled as you might imagine." Her fingers traced a stain before her, almost boomerang shaped but uneven. "The paths are straight from our standing but can curl around in unexpected ways. It is in these shapes that there is power. Close your eyes for a moment and hang to my voice."

"And if I don't? What if I get up and leave?" She shoved her chair back.

"You might not find that you like what's outside." There was no lightness in her words. "You have already taken the hardest step of your life. Everything after that will be easier."

Cait closed her eyes tight. "Like this?"

"*Relax*." The queen waited until the tension dropped out of Cait's face. "Better. Now imagine a still pool waiting forever."

"Got it."

"Do not speak. Listen." The voice was an omnipresent whisper again but patient as stone. "The surface waits and waits until a great, black stone is thrown into it. There is a crash and ripples that scatter out. You can see this, I know."

Cait imagined a flat mercury surface and the chaos that followed the stillness. It was easy.

"Now, what caused the ripples?"

"The stone."

"That is a crippled perspective. You are smarter than this now." Her hands went up before her, circle between index fingers and thumbs. "Think of instead the ripples gathering and roaring into an instant of turmoil then, as if by miracle, spitting a rock from the point where they collapse. You understand then that the ripples *caused* the rock to happen."

"No. Time doesn't do that. The rock and then the splash."

"Only from where we sit. You and me. But what if we sat outside this prison? We would see the rivers drain the seas away if we sat long enough. Or knew where to. The ripples cause the rock."

"Why are you telling me this?"

"Why do you need it to be told you? You came to me."

"No, that's not right. You *asked*. You sent Alondra for me."

"That was caused by your coming here. The asking was the result. The asking is this moment's power. The asking is what gives *you* the power, Cait. Only you could have done what I have asked."

"And what is that?"

"To bring us the *Smoking Codex* of course. You don't know how badly we needed you. *I* needed you."

Cait's eyes snapped open, and she was aware of sweat on her limbs but not that she could yet move them.

"Who is we? Not you and me."

"Let us discuss the book," the queen's smile was shaded. "You do not have it with you."

"It's in a safe place."

"There is only one safe place for it, and that is with me. You may be the means, but in your hands, it would be useless."

"Then you don't mind if I get rid of it."

The queen's perfect porcelain face tightened, but it didn't break. She stood up and pushed back from the table with a frantic scraping of the char. "The fault is mine. I forgot to be patient. You have not listened to a single word I have said."

"I have."

"My mistake, my mistake, my mistake," she repeated, motionless beneath the veil. She stood and shook herself, distress worrying her down. There was no majesty here, only a girl-woman lost in a private labyrinth of sudden realization.

"Hey," Cait stood up and reached out a hand toward her without thought. All her cool and detachedness was thrown out the window so hard it exploded. "What's wrong with you?"

The queen's now-frail arms wrapped around herself in an effort to keep from flying apart. Hunch-shouldered, she shuddered in place, standing in the heart-shaped pool of her heaped dress like black waves frozen. Like ripples.

"You see only the transaction and exchange," she whispered. "The question gives the asked the power to answer. The power is in the asking." Her breath was hot and child-scared. "I have no power, for I have given it all to you."

Then there was a word, one that Cait couldn't make out. It was as if she'd gone deaf and heard only the pounding of her pulse, rushing through useless ears. Two syllables, but she couldn't have repeated it if a gun was to her head.

". . . solo tiene poder porque lo he pedido. Ella es la ondulación y yo soy la piedra que causa la ondulación." The words erupted in a repeated catechism.

Cait understood their literal sense but not the meaning. The queen was repeating that she was the wave or that Cait was. She reached for clarity.

Who is this woman?

"Some cult mastermind you are," Cait said, slipping an arm around her. She weighed as much as a bag full of breath. "Come on. Get up."

The queen only repeated her mantra in ever-tightening circles that never quite fell upon themselves. There was always space for another verse. After a time, she stopped trying to even make sense of it, only hearing the breathless whirl of syllables, its rhythm no less driving than that of the industrial beat in the club that must have been a million miles away now.

Cait was paralyzed, holding this frailty. If either Alondra or the quiet man came through the door, what could they possibly think? That Cait somehow was able to overpower their queen? That she was a threat now?

"C'mon. You have to pull together . . . Ariela."

The queen's breathing stopped, and a sheen of sweat graced every part of her now. Veins on her temple pulsed, but that was the only part of her in motion.

"Oh shit. Don't crash out on me." She tried to imagine what the queen was on.

Junk or pills or booze or some ridiculous combination? It didn't make sense. She talked crazy but didn't act drugged.

The queen sucked in a ragged breath as if she just ripped a nail free from her palm. Her eyes opened and flitted around, taking in the scene, huge. She showed no recognition.

"¡Alejarse de mí!" she growled, deeper than possible for her small frame. Her arms pushed, reaching mostly air.

Cait pulled away as commanded but still didn't let her stand entirely on her own, not for a moment.

"Don't thank me," Cait snapped in reply. "You needed help."

The woman drew up to her full height, loose locks of hair plastered wild to her scalp and temples. The eyes beneath them were sapphire and distant, like every judge Cait could ever imagine.

"Do not talk to me of need." She smoothed out the pleats of her bodice and tugged against the top of the falling dress, causing a wave to rush through it and the pooled fabric below.

How long was this dress? How far did it go?

"Suit yourself, majesty." She paced hard around the table for seven steps, keeping herself from shoving Ariela to the ground. Something about the table scratched at her, a familiarity that she hadn't recognized at first and couldn't yet place. She looked out at the window where the lace curtains curled in upon themselves, but she couldn't tell what was wrong. It was like pushing magnets together.

"Cait, you need to understand that your quaint notions about transactional gratitude are part of the past world," she said, adjusting her hair without use of a mirror as if she could see just fine from where she stood. "Somos hijos de la roca negra ahora." Ariela's faint lisp was more pronounced now, and she said the phrase with gravity, a line of liturgy.

Not Mexican but continental Spanish. Not like her sister. If they were even that to each other.

"What does that mean?"

"Do you need a translation?"

"'We are children of the Black Rock now.' My . . . boyfriend. He taught me enough Spanish to get by."

Ariela nodded but showed only satisfaction, not pleasure. "That the ripple has caused the stone to fall, and it happened before our births. It can't be undone, only ridden and tamed."

"Like gravity?"

"After a fashion. And you are falling even as we speak." She turned from the point in space she'd contemplated, and her hair was perfect as she did. "I can catch you, but others will simply let you fall."

"So I should be thanking you?" Cait looked away from the strange woman and instead to the scarred tabletop, trying to piece together its history from the wear and tear. There was a long cut like a cleaver would make, ragged at the edges as if someone was cutting catgut amateurishly, chasing as it skittered greasily away off the cutting board and onto the tabletop. She ran her fingers across it, drawing splinters. They were real.

Wait.

"Not yet." She sighed.

"What's going on with this table?" Cait couldn't tear her eyes away as the beat welled up from the floorboards. "This is . . ." Her voice tailed off as she grabbed one of the chairs. They were mismatched, and this was the taller of them. It had a wicker back and seat and was spattered with paint and ink, perfume and smudges of ash.

"This is my chair."

"Cait, you need to listen very carefully. You think that you are powerless, that you merely copy the work of others. You borrow when you should steal."

"This is my chair."

"Believe me when I tell you that I am not the only one who recognizes your ability."

She looked up, bewildered as the beat rose and thumped, fit to shake the nails from the floor and make them dance at her feet. The whole room was coming undone. She saw the curtains, the same yellowed lace that hung in her kitchen, fluttering in an absent breeze of distant sound. She wanted to curl up and die.

"But I am the kindest of those you will meet. Also the most patient." She tugged on her fingerless gloves and was regal again. "One of these makes the other less valuable, Cait. But this is a thing I cannot control, no matter how much I actually try."

The room convulsed as every nail worked free and hung in the vibration, subject to neither gravity nor time. One of the chairs fell over and collapsed to dust. The other fell in on itself like a barn after a century of rain. The table shuddered and came apart with the splinter-scar in it growing to gird the whole and take it to pieces.

There was a blast over which Cait could clearly hear the queen asking her if she needed a car to take her home and to please take this. Something sharp pressed to her palm.

The room no longer existed if it ever had.

Cait refused the ride and trudged out of the club to call for one herself, dimly aware that she was holding onto something. She turned it over in her hand, a black and embossed business card with a number stamped into it but no name. When had she gotten that? She couldn't think any longer. Not about Rico, not about the queen, not about creepy Alondra or the quiet man. Only about one thing. That was all there was room for.

The codex doesn't have a cover. It needs one.

She dreamed about it while she held onto the card.

She got home after a cab ride back where she did nothing but stare at the streets and try to make sense of things without any trace of success. Names shown in the lights on buildings and street signs, and none of them meant any more than hesitation marks on a wrist.

Cait climbed the stairs to her loft, walked in, and marched directly to the kitchen table, sweeping it clear of all its contents in a clatter of old dishes and empty cups and ink pots. Any trace of liquid splattered to the floor, and she wouldn't look at it because she was afraid she would see meaning and a pattern there. Just as she had in the well-worn scar on the cheap tabletop. She stared at it for a moment, simply acknowledging its presence. How it exactly matched the one that had given her splinters an hour ago in audience with the queen. Anger and disgust and fear galvanized her, shocking her taut. She hissed out a breath as she upended the table with her full strength. It smashed against the nearby cupboards and slid to the floor, upside down.

The crash was anemic compared to the thump of the club's beat, but it was enough. She did the same to the chairs and ripped the curtains off the age-stained enamel curtain rod, and then she turned out the lights and didn't look back.

She worked on the cover until she couldn't stay awake any longer. She didn't even try to make it look old because it wasn't. Its age and history didn't matter, if they ever had. But it at least needed a cover.

She didn't sleep so much as she blacked out as the sun was rising.

რპ

The phone was ringing loud enough to stab through Cait's sleep and pull her out. She got up from the couch in the living area and listened for the message. One more ring. The machine clicked, and her tape-distorted voice said, "Not here. Leave a message."

The afternoon sun was bright through the laceless window.

What time was it?

"Miss MacReady, this is Detective Fellowes. I'm calling you about, ah, about Mr. Cisneros's body. If you're there, please pick up."

Her arm shot forward without thought and grabbed the handset. "I'm here. I'm here. What's happening?"

"Oh good. Listen, I wanted to ask you because you told me that your friend Rico didn't have any family up here in Los Angeles."

"He doesn't. His sister used to be here, but she moved to Tucson in, oh, '82 or so. What's . . . what's going on?"

"Where are you now?"

"What does that have to do with the body, detective?"

"Please just answer the question."

"At my apartment. I gave Trager the address."

"Well give it to me right now."

"It's on Alameda near 22nd, Cooper Building. Now what's happening?" Her words tightened, but she put that on the smoky club air and exhaustion.

"That dump? I'll be by to pick you up in twenty minutes. Be dressed and ready to go then. Don't go anywhere else, and don't talk to anyone but me."

"What's this about?"

Fellowes growled like a cornered animal. "Your friend's body was stolen from the morgue last night, Miss MacReady. The night attendant was murdered in the process. Creatively.

"Several hours before that, someone posing at his family tried to get the body released. These two facts are not unrelated."

"Oh Jesus."

"Yeah, well he's not likely to be much help in this. But I want you down to see the scene."

"What on earth for? I'm not a coroner."

"Oh, you'll know. And don't try to slip out."

☙

The pale, watery green light made the room look like a swimming pool left unattended for the season. Everything took a sickly cast: the tiles, the stainless-steel tables and cabinets, but most importantly, anything alive went half-dead, and anything dead went ghastly.

The body was set out on its back, a curly haired, pale man in greenish scrubs and a facemask. Cait tried not to think how much it reminded her of the queen's face, all eyes over the veil. His left arm was out at his side, palm up, and the other was bent at his elbow, carefully posed.

"Okay, this is familiar," Cait said. "But why?"

Fellowes said nothing but pointed. On the opposite wall, one of the refrigerated drawers was left open, tray pulled all the way out. "That's where his body was."

"But who would want to take his body? I just don't understand it."

"Look down here." The detective kneeled down and pointed at something glittering on the floor.

Cait realized there were several of them, placed carefully. Closer examination showed that they were flakes of glass, all irregular but cut into suggestive shapes. One could have been an eye, one a heart, one a hand.

The milagros again. But made of glass, just random chunks.

There was a fine powder poured into a symmetrical pattern, each of these pieces joined to the body through lines that could have been erased with a heavy breath. Someone creative might have called it a symbol.

"With ceremony," he said finally.

"Is this glass? Like the charms but glass?"

"Very good. Only a special kind of glass. Obsidian. Volcanic. You could do surgery with a piece of this cut correctly. Sharp on the molecular level, or so I hear."

"And you think whoever killed Rico killed him?"

Fellowes went stony-faced. "I didn't say anything about Cisneros having been killed."

Cait didn't look away though she wanted to. Perhaps the cold light would hide the warm flush of her face. "Oh. Yeah."

He stood and wiped the hand that had rested on the floor on last year's slacks. "Look, Miss MacReady—"

"Call me Cait. We're past formality." She stared at the body, up at the open compartment, and looked back to the policeman.

His face had softened, mostly around the eyes. The ridiculous mustache hung there like a bad joke. "We all know your friend Rico was murdered. There was no overdose. We don't know why though."

"He'd quit a couple years ago, or so I just found out."

The softness went away. "What did you learn?"

"We'll get to it," she said. "Finish your thought."

"My thought. Right. Rico was murdered because he got mixed up in something much much bigger than himself. Something with the books that we saw, books you know all too well."

She exhaled hard. "No Tomorrows," she said. "He had arranged a deal with some freaks called No Tomorrows, was going to sell them something. Or tell them where to buy it."

Fellowes shook his head but didn't smile. "This isn't a drug case. We didn't find any at his place."

"I'd heard they sold drugs," Cait played it to at least see what it got her. "Among other things."

"It's the 'among other things' that most interests me," he said. "And they don't sell so much as facilitate the sale of drugs. Coke, pills, blue star."

"Wait, stop on that last one."

"You're out of the loop. Blue star is, well, we're not entirely sure what it is. Hallucinogenic, euphoric, definitely psychoactive. A weirder angel dust."

"I don't know about that. I just drink sometimes."

His eyes flicked up and down her. "Fair enough. What *do* you know about?" His face tightened to his wrinkles. "I think I've got a right to know, and Perkins down there sure as hell does."

Cait stared into the dead man's eyes, washed out green-blue now. "They want a book," she said after a long time staring. "They want a book that I—"

She couldn't bring herself to finish the sentence, though a small part at her swelled in stung pride. She was leaving out the most important part, the part that fed her.

It's my book.

⸌⸍

Fellowes's car smelled like cigarettes and failure. Traffic on every route back had congealed into a mass of sluggish steel and frustration, last of the sunlight going down over the Hollywood hills. Everything was cheaply golden now, dripping with the stuff and sheathed in glitter, but the value was only a molecule deep. It stopped feeling real for Cait as she stared out the window. Things were stripped down to abstract shapes, even light and shadow ceasing to be meaningful other than the figures that they drew.

The air through the car window was stale and tacky, not with smog but something more cloying. Millions of others breathed it before, and it wasn't being replenished fast enough. She lay back, her head wedged between the back of the sunken seat and the door frame. The pressure on her was reassuringly real.

"If you're worried," Fellowes started to say and coughed like the stale air got him too. "If you're worried that there's charges on you, don't. You're far from the first witness who didn't offer up everything the first time I talked to them."

Cait didn't answer.

"Look, you came to the right guy here. We'll just get this wrapped up, and you'll be fine."

Every time she'd heard that, it had turned out to be a lie, so the novelty had gone out for her.

"The cops are going to protect me from this occult bullshit? Is that what Open Door does?" She was suddenly 17 again, yelling at riot cops outside the Palladium as they marched, a wall of plastic and batons. Not the same volume but the same vehemence.

The car jerked forward as Fellowes saw an opening in the other lane and lunged on it. The engine roared hollow, snapping Cait out of her rage as her head was pinned back.

"You sure picked a hell of a neighborhood," Fellowes said. "Downtown is like a sucking wound, you know. Like leprosy, and it's spreading."

"The rent is right. It's not like I live out on the street."

"Good thing. Streets aren't safe. Folks get killed all the time out here."

"Reassuring from a policeman."

"Some stuff doesn't go away when you close your eyes, kiddo."

The industrial buildings were square but shapeless as they slid up Alameda. The sun was down now, but the sky still glowed empty orange. As the sun disappeared, a wind came up, and trash blew along the streets, bouncing off gutters like addled animals.

"Here, right?"

"Yeah, yeah." Cait shook off the lethargy and unsnapped the seat belt, not realizing how tight it had been until it was gone.

"So it's the book they want? That's what you said." He slammed the door with something akin to eagerness. Wind ran through his curly hair, and he reached for a cigarette.

"Thought you were quitting."

"Trying to. Not having a lot of luck." He marched to the door and waited. "Let's not drag this out."

She pulled out the big, bitten key and worked the lock.

"Your partner said Open Door is the weirdo cases. How bad is this one?"

"Depends who you are. For your friend and Perkins, pretty bad. Probably for a bunch of other people we haven't even found yet."

She tried not to think about how many bodies were tied up with No Tomorrows. The door came open with a dry coughing click. "Yeah, but how weird?"

"How weird you want it?" He leered like it was the only thing he could do. "This city is diseased. Sometimes people catch that and do their own thing with it. People like No Tomorrows? They spread it for fun.

"Now let's stay focused on the book."

"Yeah, okay."

The stairs up went long and smelled like the urine of ghosts. Cait paused at the door, Fellowes two steps behind her.

It hung open, just a crack. Through that crack seeped a smell, something that Cait had never known. It smelled of hot metal and dust, of crackling smoke, but all that was miles away, just the echo of it. It was like the ringing in her ears if she thought of it, suddenly omnipresent.

"The door's open," she hissed.

"No roommate?" Fellows asked as his hand went to the holster under his jacket just below his heart. He came out with a snub-nosed revolver, not a big cop gun but something small.

"No. And I locked it when we left."

Fellowes pushed past her without a sound.

"You smell that?" she asked.

"What? The flowers? Yeah."

"No, something else. Dry and electric."

"Stop using coke. That stuff fucks with your nose and everything else."

She didn't have the temper to correct him as he pushed the door open further and slid into the apartment.

For the next five minutes, neither of them said a word, only Fellowes using hand gestures to bring her along or hold her back while he checked out a room. The apartment itself seemed just the same as she'd left it, other than the kitchen table and chairs having been replaced and stood back up. She couldn't remember if she'd done that in a sleep haze or not. Something told her "no" to that.

Fellowes gave a second glance to the sturdy, welded bookcases along the brick walls. Cait wondered why. Nobody could hide in those or even behind them.

Her apartment felt removed, alien, every space within it pregnant with threat. It was someone else's home now. Someone else's work space, filled with another's essence, rendered strange by a new distance. The posters and flyers tacked and taped to the walls were names she recognized, but their meaning had been shorn from them.

The cop ahead of her swung his arm quickly, pivoting on his foot as he came around a corner. He swept her bedroom quickly, the last room in the place to be surveyed, but found nothing. Fellowes stuffed the pistol back into the holster in a kind of sad frustration.

The smell never went away. It was in every room now. Even here where she slept. The same scent, like something marking territory, and hers was all but pushed out.

Fellowes turned back to her. He was still lit with a piercing energy that burned through his eyes, all shot blue. "There's. Nobody. Here. Just us."

"But someone did come through the door. I didn't imagine that."

"Nah, of course not." He looked at his fingernails, spread out before him, and reached into his loose coat pocket and pulled out a pair of gloves, patterned and tooled just like the driving gloves her dad used to wear when driving that Jaguar around the hills in Riverside. Fellowes put them on with purpose.

"Now let's talk about what you *did* imagine."

"I don't understand."

He let the tension spill out of him. "Hey, forget it. Just a bad joke, okay?"

Cait was aware of her right hand cradling her left elbow like a scared little kid. "Okay, okay. Yeah." She stood up straighter, trying to shake it off, and wrinkled her nose at the smell. "You really don't notice that?"

"What? Dingy flop? Nah. I've smelled worse." He marched out to the hallway again and stopped in front of the bookshelf.

"I'm, ah, I'm just going to light a candle and try to clear this smell."

"Knock yourself out." He fingered some of the books, hard enough to make them move on the loosely packed shelves. "Nice collection."

"It's for work," she called back from the kitchen now. She rummaged in a drawer for the big, wooden matches, struck one on the box, and took it with care over to the four-wick blacking lamp.

Gonna smoke like a tire fire but should clear out the smell. Did one of my jars of perfume break?

She tried to figure out which combination of perfumes might make this scent but came up empty as she carried the lamp to a side table in the living area, well away from curtains or anything else that might easily catch.

Fellowes lingered at the hall doorway, just watching her. "That's a hell of a thing. You find that at Satan's garage sale?"

"It's Tibetan. And I'm not in your house, making fun of your stuff."

"Yeah, I—" He was cut off by the phone's metallic ring.

Fellowes waited, watching her. Cait looked away.

"Who's calling?" he asked. "You expecting anyone?"

"The hell should I know? I'll let the machine get it."

He held her still with the same silent hand signal that he'd used to usher her through the apartment.

The phone rang, weak at the end like the ringer was dying.

"How long until your machine picks up?" He was agitated, maybe craving another cigarette, but Cait knew better. She'd seen the look in him that she'd seen from other men wanting something of her.

Only he wasn't after the physical but something else.

"Fourth ring. Calm down."

"Don't tell me what to do."

They stood near the table, in range of the answering machine's speaker. The phone rang a fourth time, and there was a click as the machine started. Cait's voice came out, impatient.

She was aware of his tight and controlled breathing.

"Miss MacReady, this is Detective Trager with Open Door at LAPD."

She heard Fellowes's breath stop.

Cait didn't turn her head to look at her apparent captor, but she could hear his teeth on edge against one another. He vibrated, a lit fuse and burning fast.

"It's very important that you pick up right now. There's been some developments in the case, and I need—"

She snapped up the phone and said, "Yes, I'm here and—!"

That's all she could say before the phone was slapped out of her hand.

"Useless twist." There wasn't even real anger behind it but some vague irritation, dog shit on the sole of his new shoes.

The handset went flying across the room.

"Miss MacReady?!" Trager's voice came from the other side of the moon.

"Your partner is here! He's threatening me!"

She didn't see the shove coming and just smacked into the throw rug on the floor, seeing only stars.

"Oh shit! Oh shit! Get out of there! I'll . . . !" The voice sounded as if from an ant now, something laughably powerless as Fellowes pressed down on the phone cradle and ended the call.

"That could have been smoother. That's my fault," he said wearily. "Now get up."

"Are you going to hurt me?" Cait cringed at the weakness of the question, but it blurted out like blood from a fresh wound.

"You mean am I going to hurt you *more*, right? No. Not too much. I'm just the finder." He tightened his glove. His jacket hung open, and his holster was plain to see, but he didn't even bother grabbing at the gun.

That last thought bit at Cait more than anything as she turned her weight beneath herself, so she could get up. Very slowly.

"You aren't even going to guess why, are you?"

"The why isn't really important," she said. "Just how you get what you want is."

"The fuck does that mean? God you really are full of yourself." He coughed a seal bark of a laugh. "Look, let's just do this fast." His face went dead as he curled his fingers in sequence, warming up. "Get me the book, and I promise you that I won't lay another hand on you."

"Be specific."

"You know which fucking one. Snap to."

There was a crackle somewhere in the outer hallway like a cellophane cigarette wrapper being crunched up, only louder and longer, more persistent. Like the smell, the more she thought about it, the more present it was.

Behind that sound, there was only silence and Fellowes's tight breathing. He was on something, and it wasn't nicotine this time.

Her right hand was close enough to her pocket that she could get her keys. Fellowes wouldn't be the first man she'd punched them with, but he was the first cop.

"Why?" She asked without moving, only her fingertips touching the brass and steel. "This doesn't seem like LAPD policy."

"Hah. You'd be surprised." He couldn't help but laugh at his own joke.

"Maybe not. Rampart cops are the worst."

"Oh, that's right. You were a little punk rocker. Like that matters for shit."

The keys comforted her as she wiggled them between her fingers.

"This is business but not police business."

She breathed in, and the smell still lingered, but more than that, she was flooded with the memory of the meeting at the club when Tácito made the sign of the crossed eyes and the palm. Just like Fellowes had done over Rico's body.

"It's No Tomorrows business," she said with a weight.

"Hey, if you say so." She could hear the shrug and the crackle behind it, something pushing at a door and finding no purchase but still trying. "I got a request to find a book. It's not one we got. It's not one anyone's got.

"But it turns out that people think it's one you got. So how about it, sweetheart? Where's this *Smoking Codex*? Sounds like money to me."

"Let me get up, and I'll show you."

"That's better. I knew you could be trained."

She stood up with care, hand withdrawn from her pocket now, and the tips of the keys between her first knuckles like tiny extra digits. "Over this way." She indicated the welded bookcase with the point of her chin. "If I'd known that was what you'd wanted I'd have told you."

"Sure you would. Walk." His eyes were on the bookshelf now. She could see that clearly as she passed in front of him to lead.

No way he'll turn in time.

"Yeah, some dump you got here, but who gives a shit if—"

He didn't get to finish the sentence as Cait threw a cross punch with the keys right into Fellowes's throat. He made a choking gasp and lost whatever he was going to say next. Eyes wide with shock, he still focused on her in disbelief.

She made two steps for the door before the smell and the crackling hit her. Then she saw what was making it.

The figure stood just under her height but was probably taller, for it hunched waist to shoulders as if even existing was a terrible burden, barely hefted. Its body was the black that would happen if shadows could cast shadows. Smoke emanated from its body, every surface but for the face.

Not emanating. Coalescing.

It solidified out of smoke that wasn't there, some force pulling this thing into existence, forming the body of a man but made from darkness. Beneath the shifting smoke, she could see structures like bones, glowing in a sourceless kind of x-ray radiation. They were the shadows of a skeleton.

She looked at the thing, and it pulled itself up to a more natural posture with effort. Familiarity tugged at her, but she refused to think of what it suggested.

Tiny metallic objects went around it in a pulsing and changing cluster, constellations with their own orbits drawing figures pregnant in meaning and endlessly repeating.

Above the hunched shoulders hung a slender face, no trace of the phantom skeleton beneath it, only a mirrored surface like subtly rippling mercury. Smoky wisps of hair ringed it, tossing in a wind without origin. She knew the face and its contours, even without identity. She'd held it, stroked it with her own fingers, kissed its—

"Dumb bitch!" Fellowes growled before the blow landed. She crumpled as a star burst somewhere just off her spine, above her pelvis. "What are you even staring at?"

Kidneys. Cheating bastard.

She couldn't string a thought together after that. She felt only the blue fire of the pain, radiating from the fist-sized spot.

"Oh, fuck me." Fellowes's voice lit up with fear now. "What the fuck is this shit?"

She opened her eyes and craned her head to see the thing step into the room and Fellowes backing away with it, features pulled tight into a rictus of weak challenge.

The thing couldn't answer his question. It reached a hand toward him, shedding thick, languid smoke that just rolled off and fell to the ground.

"Fuck off. It's mine."

He whipped the gun out of its holster and splayed out three shots into its center mass. It worked as well as shooting smoke possibly could. The thing remained unruffled, perhaps even unaware that it had been shot. But it did come to a stop in front of him. Fellowes's eyes were down, and he shook in place, a fish out of water and out of energy to fight. His breath stilled, tight inhales without exhales, getting tighter each time.

Someone else followed the thing in and closed the door behind.

Tácito stood gracefully, just off the doorway, a smile of curiosity on his face as he regarded Fellowes. He wore no shoes, silent as smoke. In his left hand, he held out the same glittering dagger he'd used at the salon. It flashed in motion, finishing a sign drawn in the air, and if Cait concentrated enough, she could just barely see the last traces of it scratched out. The angles of it tugged at her, something only half remembered.

Fellowes stood just out of arm's reach of the thing, but if it took another step, he'd be able to hug it. The shadow stood in front of him, only waiting. The constellation in orbit around it flashed like tiny, silver fish, crossing over one another, and in that moment, Cait accepted whose body stood in the room, whose corpse acted as its scaffold or the bridge from another reality to the one she knew. They were permanently joined now, and this thing that used to be Rico was the conduit from imagination to something more.

"What the fuck is this? You aren't supposed to be here." Fellowes's hard eyes never left the thing, staring into a point where its face would be.

Then where was *he supposed to be?*

It was almost too much. Cait wanted to crumble away and let the nightmare end, but she knew it would be there even when her eyes were closed. She could only watch as whatever Rico had become held the cop in place, but it wasn't like him saving her. Not now.

Tácito waved with the point of the knife, indicating for Fellowes to drop the gun. His smile shown as bright as his eyes dark.

"And if I don't?"

"Lo ciento," he replied without sorrow at all. His smile never flagged. His voice was clipped and rough, false apology coming out sandpaper harsh.

Cait looked on as Fellowes continued staring, head fixed but body limp.

His eyes widened now, irises flattening to black and empty discs. Whatever he was on consumed him. "I can't. What is this? I'm looking behind and in front of . . . this . . . this hasn't . . . happened yet . . ."

"Ahora," Tácito said.

The creature reached out and put its hand into Fellowes's head, his flesh was meaningless. The smoking fingers pushed past skin and bone and whatever else. They hesitated for a second, stuck on something, before sinking past the second knuckles. The hand held there, and the fingers wriggled for a second or two.

Fellowes's body went rigid and quivered, mouth opened in a scream but nothing came out. Only the faintest of rasping, dry gurgling. The thing pulled its hand away, and as it did, it seemed to distort Fellowes's face, not simply pulling his skin but bending and stretching his face and skull like warm butter.

His mouth stayed open but stopped issuing any sound. Then he fell backward, slumping against the wall, limp and boneless.

The skeleton stood there waiting.

Tácito held his left hand before his face, palm out. "Lo mismo para usted." He brought his hand out before him, curling and unfolding it in a wave, beckoning with the grace of practice and intention.

The smoking creature turned toward Cait, but she didn't look at it. She couldn't. She knew the more she did, the more she would see Rico in it, and in time, she wouldn't be able to look away.

"You have to let me get it," she said. Her own voice sounded small, making conditions that were laughable on their face.

"Bien," he replied. He held the knife up and out, tipping the point twice, indicating her toward the bookshelf. His eyes were as hungry as Fellowes's, devouring titles on spines.

Would he even know the right one?

She took a step, reminding herself how to do so. Adrenalin and fear still surged through her, to her fingers shaking uselessly.

Maybe the thing still watched, but she wouldn't look.

Fellowes made a baby's noise, soft and undulating vowel sounds.

"Ahora." Tácito repeated, less patient this time.

She couldn't take the risk. He wasn't going to be fooled by anything less than the genuine article.

If my book is even that.

She walked slowly away from the bookshelf and saw as Tácito raised an eyebrow.

"Oye. La estancería." He pointed at the bookshelf with the knife's tip. It glittered in the reflected lamp light.

"No está aqui," she replied.

He grunted a response that she didn't quite catch, but he kept his pet creature away, so he must have understood.

She bent over and pulled the cushion off the couch. It had belonged to her grandmother, who'd lived during Prohibition and had a taste for gin that could never be satisfied. Beneath the cushions, hidden compartments defied all but expert search.

"Bien, bien."

A flash of pride crept through her at the sight of the book. Here it was, something she'd created at the center of this whole web of events. Hers.

She'd been asked. And the power had been given to her by asking.

"Oye! Cait!" Tácito snapped. As he did, the thing rustled, accompanied by a faint musicality from the jingling milagros orbiting it.

She turned and held the book in her hands, opening the modest cover to the frontispiece. In it, she saw details and drawings that she now recognized as being mirrored in the tattoos that Tácito and everyone in No Tomorrows had worn. Cait struggled with the reality of that for a second as she showed him the book, open and uncovered.

"Es verdad," he said just over a whisper. The knife hand dropped in reverence as his eyes went wide and dark. "Sombra y silencio." He spoke the phrase with his left hand in front of his mouth, tattooed back shown to Cait.

Fellowes made another noise, this one more organized, less helpless. Like a man waking from years of sleep.

"Dámela ahora." He snapped his fingers. The reverence left his voice, now only orders as hard as concrete. The flickering flames of the lamp lit his face, making the creases deep and black. His slicked hair still shone.

I have been asked. I am the stone.

Cait stood and waited. "Not without a promise of safety."

His eyes went greedy and tight. "¿Promesa?" He laughed, and it meant as much as the words he'd said to Fellowes. His hand swept again before his lips. "Your life is over, little Cait. Change is coming to your world."

"English? But . . ."

He spat contempt. "I wanted to make sure you understood."

She didn't move and instead glanced at the lamp and its four flames, each fat and flickering. It wasn't that far. Not even the thing could make it to her before she could do what she had in mind.

"Now do as I say. Give me it." He held his hand out.

Fellowes made another sound, anger bubbling beneath it.

Tácito's frown mocked her. "Oh. You think the queen can save you? That ridiculous little Spaniard?" He shook his head, and the grin he wore had no mirth or mercy in it. "Make things easy for yourself. Be easy, and you can continue selling your little books to whomever." The contempt wrapped around his words like a snake crushing a bird. It was all she could hear. But the contempt wasn't just for Cait.

"Spaniard? I don't understand."

"Enough." He'd gone to gloating. She recognized the satisfaction in his voice and would've even if it were in Spanish still. As with Khan, he was high on his own confidence. "If we were to talk about what you don't understand, we'd never finish. Now do this. Give me the book, so we can end—"

She didn't linger about what he'd said and instead vaulted over the couch to get within reach of the lamp.

"No!" he shouted behind her.

She felt its heat and yellow-orange light play over her hands and the pages as she held them open, very close, but not enough to smoke. The tallow smell was a balm to her.

Cait only looked at him, keeping her arms rigid, though the heat burned her hand. Yesterday's welt was a red chasm across it. She wished she'd chosen better but wasn't even going to risk changing hands now.

"Call it off!" she ordered. "Call it off. Or I burn the book, and the queen gets nothing!"

Tácito chuckled, and Cait's heart sank at the rippling laughter. "You think that this is for the queen?" The sneer soured him. "Don't be a child like her. Give—"

The report of Fellowes's pistol boomed and cut the phrase dead. Gunpowder smoke billowed, and Cait gasped against it. Her hand faltered for a second, and one of the page corners dipped to where the flame could lick at it.

Tácito shouted, more in outrage than pain. He issued a sound that felt like a prelude to a longer phrase, rich with expectation.

Fellowes grunted, thick with drool, and shot again. The second shot sounded wetly into the other man's throat, syllable to gurgle. Nothing between his jaw and chest worked any longer. His head sagged forward as his body crumpled.

The knife made a clean ringing as it hit the floor, and even though it was made of glass, it didn't shatter or even chip.

Cait cried but only at the heat eating her hands. The codex slipped from her fingers, burning as it fell face down to the floor. She kicked at it with her foot, scuffing it further and smothering any flame.

She couldn't look away this time. The thing said nothing, only finished the job it had started, sinking both hands into the sitting Fellowes's cranium like clay to be worked. He fired his last shot into its heart, bullets doing as little damage as they would to a shadow.

Fellowes couldn't make a sound. His face went through permutations, an array of funhouse mirror reflections. Smoke poured off the wrists of the thing and finally out of Fellowes's eyes and nose as if he'd been hollowed out and filled with it.

Tácito's body heaved in place but without the strength needed to get up. His hand splayed, trying to reach the knife less than a foot away.

Cait grabbed it without thought. He'd used it to control the thing, and a part of her said that he'd used it to even summon the thing, and in that moment, she remembered everything she'd written about the ritual. All of it bullshit, but the truest kind.

Cold to the touch, it sang in her hand, and she felt it slice the air.

The thing, satisfied in its work, left the cop's corpse in the corner. It turned to her without malice or motivation, merely waiting for another command.

She held the knife before her as the smoking thing simply existed, impossibly. Rico's bones anchored it here. She could recite the summoning ceremony, even the name of the white obsidian blade used to guide it, but not how to send the thing away.

But it couldn't stay. She couldn't allow it.

"You're released," she said weakly.

The thing remained unmoved. Stars glimmered around the vapor-shrouded bones.

"Go on!" She slashed with the knife, but it cut only air.

She brought the knife back, suddenly nauseous at realization. There was a dead cop and a gangster, or whatever the hell Tácito was, and no explanation for the thing. Tears welled up in her but not tears of helplessness or fear. What they were didn't have a name but hung somewhere between anger and sorrow, and all of it was recognition.

The mirrored face of the thing caught her eye finally. The contours of Rico's features were nearly erased by whatever force had brought him here. The face was a reflecting pool but distorted such that she had a view of the room and herself in it from all angles at once. It wasn't complete though. Any time she came close to it, another detail in another angle hooked her eye, and everything shook and refocused around that. She could stay there forever if she let herself. She wanted to.

The thing's hand rose, phantom bones trapped in its smoke.

The scent of it, that ghost trace, came on ammonia strong. Cait pulled herself free of the mirror pool as surely as if it had been smashed by a stone.

She slashed again, catching the fingers at the knuckle, just over where the hand itself ended. The severed digits smoked before pattering to the floor, leaving only blackened and withered bones.

If the thing was hurt, it gave no sign.

Cait let the tears burn as she stared at the knucklebones on the floor, unnaturally even where the knife had sliced.

Without looking up, she gutted the thing, slicing upward through the ribs and one of the arms held before it. Smoke of purple and blue and black roiled around the slice in space. It appeared a hurricane in two dimensions, stretched out and curled around itself as the flat tendrils crossed over one another as naturally as water flowing uphill.

Her slicing stroke razored across the top of the thing's skull, which fell over and tumbled to the floor. Smoke boiled up and *inward* from its cranium as if unable to escape some grasping force.

Again and again and again, she cut until the thing wasn't there any longer, only the softly dissipating vapor and a collection of impossibly cut bones with Rico's milagros scattered in between them, some sliced straight in half.

അ

She had no more tears, only smoke-streaked tracks on her face. The thing's bones were dissolving now, leaving that smell burned into the rug. She'd have to burn that when this was all over. Gently, she picked out the charms from the midden, wincing as the fresh edge of one of them caught her on her fingertip and drew blood. She smiled at the fairness of it and let it bleed.

The book waited for her, still face down on the floor. She turned it over and winced again at the burned page. The whole of it smelled of soot and the fuel of the blacking lamp, which still burned.

"Nothing permanent."

The relief in the phrase evaded her.

She closed the book and held it close with one hand while she looked for a place to stash the knife. She went through the closet, throwing jackets out over her shoulder until she found the long black one, now faded to a smoggy grey, which she'd sewn a long pocket in the lining years ago for contraband that she'd never carried but wanted to. That was before she found that bouncers didn't give a shit what you brought as long as you didn't wave it under their nose. Cait pulled the jacket on with a shrug.

She knelt to work the sheath free from Tácito's hip. His dead weight shifted, and she knocked herself over trying to get away. She held her breath the entire time and, even after, had to breathe through her mouth to keep from gagging on the smell. He was already going cold, but he wasn't using the damn thing, so she just pushed ahead and did it. The leather-covered blade slid into that long pocket now, and she tied the belt tight.

Dead cop and a dead crook. Can't be calling the law in on this one. They can't help, anyways.

She looked up the number, rummaging through the now-clean kitchen to find it tacked to a wall with a nail she didn't recognize. She ripped the card off and dialed the number. She couldn't run away, but maybe she didn't need to.

The call was brief, a voice telling Cait, "She's down on Alameda, waiting," and nothing more. Cait couldn't bring herself to ask how Alondra was there already.

Cait blew out the lamp and told herself she'd be back. The room went dark and didn't care if she returned.

The car waited.

ঌ৶

Sick and steady light from the sodium lamps offered little relief against the darkness of Alameda. The moisture had run in from the Santa Monica coastline and swathed the sky, so the city light bounced around and made for a yellow half-light that only tricked you into thinking you could see. Fellowes's car sat parked tight in front, four doors of bureaucratic lowballing.

Another car, parked halfway down the block, turned on its big, round headlights. The engine started, and a liquid purr rolled down the street toward Cait, just like the car did.

No Tomorrows was here already. Despite calling only moments ago.

Screeching rubber cut down the avenue as a third car came careening around 23rd and onto Alameda like trying to cross a collapsing bridge before it all fell apart. Another generic and unassuming sedan, similar to Fellowes's, wavered down the road with speed. Its headlights passed over Cait, and it corrected course, racing right toward her.

The other car kept its slow roll and would reach her first quite easily. It rolled invulnerable, the baddest thing in sight. The streetlight poured off its glossy black fenders and roofline: an old car with a chrome grill and a profile that showed strength in those curves. The hood looked a mile long as it came to Cait like an oil slick hitting a pristine beach.

Last year's sedan came to a skittering halt some distance away. The door flung open and detective Trager's stout silhouette leaned in the space behind the car body and the open door. Light glinted at the end of his grasp.

"LAPD! All of you freeze!"

The Mercury's back door opened and hung there.

"Miss MacReady?! Are you all right?"

Cait stared at the waiting car. The smell of cigarette smoke and roses poured out the passenger compartment. An inked hand rested on the window sill of the driver's side, a woman's hand. Alondra's. The tattoos were as unique as a fingerprint off a corpse.

"It's okay, detective. But you're too late."

Trager flicked on the searchlight, pointing it right at the hulking shape of the Mercury. The hand on the driver's side went to the middle finger and held it long enough for him to see it clearly.

They weren't going to scatter when the cops came.

"You in the car! Come out with your hands where I can see them!"

"You can see them just fine!" Alondra's voice called back. She waved the middle finger enough to be sure.

"You wait here," Cait said to the waiting car. "I'll be right back." She turned toward Trager's vehicle and took a step, hands out at her sides, book still in her left. "Your partner went bad," she said.

"Been bad for a long time, just couldn't get solid proof. That's why I told you to talk to me and me only. Couldn't even do that right," he muttered at the end. His face tangled up in disgust and worry.

She took another couple steps and stopped, close enough that she wouldn't have to yell but far enough away that she wouldn't be tempted to run to him. "He came to me, detective. Wasn't much I could do about it."

"You could have told me the whole story at Rico's house. Whatever that whole story was."

What? That I wrote a book to summon a god not yet born? That I'm some kind of goddamn priestess?

"Wouldn't have mattered. No Tomorrows isn't something one cop's gonna stop."

"It's not bigger than you, Cait."

"Tell him to turn that light off," Alondra growled. "¡O vamos a disparar!" She laughed, pure mean.

Cait could feel the urge to beg him to stay, but she choked it back. It would just get him killed, and she'd still end up at the same place. "Go home, detective. There isn't anything more you can do here."

She turned to leave, scraping on the asphalt as she did, and stopped. "But you're right. It's not bigger than me. Just about my size."

"Go home, piggy," Alondra teased. "This isn't your business."

"You don't have to do this," he pleaded. "Whatever happened, there's a way out."

Cait laughed and shook her head. "I may not have to do this, but I sure as hell am going to. Just go and clean up the apartment. Guy from No Tomorrows and your partner did one another. I'll tell you the story when I get back."

Trager shook his head. "Freeze right there," he warned. It was a desperate last shot, but he took it anyway. "And you all wait for backup to get here."

"Just leave now before they get tired of you, detective. You did your best. But Open Door isn't going to get this one."

Cait watched Trager invisibly wrestling on a five count before holstering his gun. "I hope you know what you're doing."

She shrugged, trying fatalism on for size. "Not a clue, but it's got to be done."

A cold, moist wind kicked up as Trager piled back into his car, and it pulled away slowly. Cait turned to see Alondra waving farewell to him as he did. Her black fingernails shone and glinted like glass on the street. The last steps to the open door went fast, melting into a single breath. The leather seat sighed as Cait sat down. The slim length of the knife reassured her as much as the flat book she held on her lap.

"Take me to the queen," she said.

"Nowhere else to go," Alondra replied.

Cait slid and held on as the Mercury went on with a low-throated roar, through the night fog and the ghostly nebulae of light orbiting the lamp posts. The onramp to I-10 was empty, and the car surged ahead, all power and steel weight.

∽

The only house on the street, it sat up the hill from a row of tall cypress trees, standing like a line of huge and irregular grave markers by the sidewalk. From the street, only the wall of crooked foliage was visible. Behind it, the grounds were bare but for the abandoned stumps of long-cut trees, knife handles sticking out of a back but buried deep. The house behind them was tall and gothic in proportion, all lit from below, making it seem twice as tall.

"Our stop," Alondra said, her first words since the car had started moving. "La reina espera."

"She can wait a little bit longer." Cait didn't move just yet.

The back doors locked with a snap, and Cait knew that she wouldn't be able to open them and that reaching for the latch was the wrong decision. Alondra stood motionless, her twin nooses hanging to either side of her neck, hair pulled tight across her scalp. She swallowed hard and asked, "What you said about Tácito? Was that true?" She watched Cait intently through the rear view mirror, gaze picking past the surface, looking for a lie to dig into.

Cait wondered if they shared a connection more than simply the queen and decided to leave out the details of the creature and everything else. "Two bullets. One in the throat. Wasn't much for me to do about it."

"And he killed the other cop? This bad cop?"

"I guess Tácito had been waiting in my place for a while, looking for the book. He jumped the cop, razored him, but couldn't do it fast enough to get away clean."

Her black eyes softened. Alondra either decided that this was the truth or that she wasn't ever going to get it. "Mm-hmm." The murmur was blank but stitched with suspicion. She put the car into park and clattered down on the brake. "And the dead cop, what did he want from you?"

"The book. Someone else is after it. Didn't say who. Seemed like something he was hired on, not for himself. Maybe they were working together. The cop seemed to recognize him but was surprised all the same."

Alondra's cheeks flushed with irritation. Her lips went tight, and she nodded as if confirming a long-held suspicion. "That is not welcome news." She hissed out an irritated sigh that went to her shoulders. "I told my sister that her patience wouldn't serve her well." She turned and looked into Cait, eyes only a glimmer in the green dash lights. They were hungry.

"Her patience did just fine. I'm here." Cait reached for the handle of the door, a smooth fetish of metal in her hand. "Should we go?"

Alondra's eyes were empty now, her words dead weight as she said, "Yes. Go to *her*."

Cait didn't move, instead trying to figure out the tone in her voice.

Rejection? Resignation? Concern?

"You're not related at all, are you?"

"Was it the blue eyes?" Alondra snapped.

"Not hardly." Cait laughed and hoped it bit. "It's the *everything*, woman. She's a child. Maybe a magic child but a child. You're more real than that."

"You should be careful."

"We're way past careful." Cait leaned forward, remembering her fire before the meeting at the Last Prayer and called some of that back. "You're holding things together, aren't you? You remind me of my boyfriend's sister. It's always on the oldest when things come apart. And she's cool on the front but barely hanging together on the inside."

Alondra lost her voice for a long time. "The queen has her tasks, and I have mine," the words were heavy, gravity like an oncoming train hollering down the tracks.

"Tácito, he called her a 'Spaniard.' And while she's . . ."

"Bolillo," she said and snapped her lips across her teeth. "This is a rude way to say—"

"White bread. I get it."

Alondra sagged a little, rolling her head forward in resignation, but her shoulders stayed squared. "Blood is not the only way to make family. Ariela is my sister. No matter what either of us does, we share that. But the king, he is *not* our brother."

"Then who—"

"Enough talking. Go." Alondra unlocked the door by switch and stared straight ahead until Cait moved.

Whatever fog crept in the lower part of the basin didn't reach up here. The stars above them were bright but watery still, twinkling with agitation. The sky pulsed, alive with them, even the faint structure of the Milky Way visible. Cait tried to remember the last time she'd seen it and couldn't, not even as a child. Riverside might have hills to climb, but it was still in the wash of crappy air that started in LA and reached all the way down the San Gabriels to the ocean and maybe even the Mexican border.

Huge and gaunt with age, the house had a Victorian foundation riddled with detail and oddity. The archway to the house's atrium cut an asymmetrical profile, distractingly so, fashioned out of wrought iron that seemed to move even without a wind to drive it. The roofline worked an angle that was sheer murder, poised as a dagger thrust up to the sky's belly.

All the windows were veiled, showing smudgy amber light in only a few.

"You first," Alondra said to no one.

The front door hung open, and an oblong of yellow light led Cait inside. The stairs beneath her feet gave just a little, like taut muscle. The place was nobility collapsing in on itself, watered down generation after generation until the blood was too thin to support its own history or future. It was the last in line.

Inside, the house vibed empty, though the distant sound of sad music played upstairs, Spanish lyrics she couldn't make out. All the edges of things were fanciful and curlicued, details that tried to add up to a whole but could not.

"This way, my Cait," came the queen's voice from a room on this floor. The lilt in the voice tugged at her.

Alondra stood on the threshold, unwilling to go further.

"Aren't you coming?" Cait asked, her own question sounding stupid to herself.

"I don't go into the house," she replied. "Never fear. I will be close." She made a hand motion and urged her inside.

Though getting tired of being ordered around, she let it slide. The room waited for her to cross it. The furniture must have been more than a century old, which would have made this one of the older standing houses in Los Angeles. It was easy to forget that this city had a past before the twentieth century since so much of it seemed to be in constant construction or mid-modern dilapidation like it had been dumped out of an assembly kit and put together and then discarded out of manic boredom.

The light came from the back room, and Cait walked toward it. She made an effort to touch nothing. It felt like a museum, a place made to look lived in but only feeling cold and neat. It was a shrine to a time long ago gone, waiting for restoration.

Ariela the Queen waited on a red velvet couch made of the same material as her booth in the Last Prayer had been. She wore another pooled black dress: this one nearly without ornament, just complexity in stitching and design. The detail was subtle but unmistakable. In the dim light, the individual threads teased not only at her silhouette but at signs and sigils that seemed to rewrite themselves with her every movement. The datura tattoo on Ariela's chest expanded with an inhale of anticipation. Her skin was flat in this light, almost chalky. A smile hid behind her veil, Cait just knew it.

She tried to remember her own words about the queen in the car, but that was forever ago and no longer mattered.

"You have brought the book. That's so wonderful." She rested a perfect and graceful hand on the velvet cushion and patted. "Please sit with me, so we can read it."

"Ariela, you should know that Tácito, he . . ."

"Sit, please."

"But he's dead."

Her eyes showed no sadness or remorse but instead the quiet reassurance of a confirmation. "There are many kinds of death, Cait." Her voice went hollow and whispery.

She sat down on the sofa, martial, rigid, not soft at all. "But I think that he . . . he wanted the book for himself, not for you."

"That may be. He was not patient." She rested a hand on Cait's own, cool as ivory. The red nails glittered like scales of some great snake. "For all there is of time, things must happen in their proper arrangement. Many in No Tomorrows do not understand this like I do."

Cait shifted in the seat but let Ariela's hand stay. "You talk like you're not with them." She couldn't bring herself to ask about what Alondra had said.

The veil didn't move with her intake of breath. "No Tomorrows is a family, Cait. It might be difficult for you to see. And can any family claim real harmony?"

"Not when they're more than three people," Cait joked.

"And maybe not even then." She traced the cover, pulling a pattern out where there was none to be seen. "My family is interested in this world, you understand. They want to make their money and sell drugs and peddle influence, all of it very unseemly." Her brow furrowed at that: disgust or pity, Cait wasn't sure.

"You're talking about crime."

Ariela's eyes went upward and held there a moment before locking to Cait's. "Do you know what crime is?"

"Breaking the law?"

"Crime, Cait, is nothing more than the changing of the way things are." Her voice bent itself to a haughty nobility, one above the law and doing as she saw fit. "The theft of money. Murder. Tak*ing*. Crime and magic are not so dissimilar. They are both the taking of what you want. Desire."

"And what do you desire?"

"I once walked the same path that they did. But I was unafraid to use the knowledge I learned along the way to ascend."

"Magic again."

"I'm talking about knowledge, Cait. And it was knowledge that I didn't understand until I shed the pursuit of gain in this world."

After you'd gotten what you wanted.

Ariela's hand moved to the book and its faintly rippled leather cover. It seemed so plain and humble under her immaculate fingers and the black lace across her the back of her hand. But it seemed right, as if shaped and proportioned for her when Cait knew it to be nothing more than coincidence. The roughness of the cover suggested detail and meaning that could be poured over for hours, days, and it would never all be reckoned, just an endless fold of Ariela's dress. That was the cover she had in her head.

"I sought knowledge for its own sake. I became a daughter of the Black Rock, of the silence and shadow that waited there. Sombra y silencio."

Cait fell into the lilting lisp in the queen's voice before her head hurt. She couldn't figure out the source of the pain. The music upstairs grew louder, plaintive but unyielding. "And . . . and how did your family take to that?"

"How would yours? How would yours when they didn't understand?" Her voice hesitated, both in simmering frustration and resignation long past caring. "I can still distract them, scare their opponents, let them bleed out their string of crimes. I can even teach Alondra and Tácito some of these tricks." Now contempt filled her voice. "So stupid. But you still want to tell them, you know?

"You want someone who understands, someone you can share this with." There was a longing there, not for mere blood but for something deeper even than that.

Cait pretended to know. Her family was one thing but acceptance was another. She'd passed off so many fake books that the rejection of her original work had always cut.

But in the presence of the queen, that wound healed. And Cait didn't know how to accept that. Not with all it meant. It was too great a load. Her pulse thundered through her body in exertion.

"But you and I, we will tell them in a way that cannot be ignored any longer. They will realize that my pathetic tricks and sleights of hand are just that. They will realize the truth behind all of them, and they will understand.

"Just like you have come to understand."

Cait clenched her teeth and shook herself, but the pain didn't subside.

"You are so close, Cait," she said. Ariela's voice remained calm and soft as her friend Lucille's the night after the clinic, that horrible never-ending night that could still cut to the center of her even in memory.

"I can't."

The book slid from Cait's grasp. "You can. You are so close to seeing." The queen took the book and opened it between them, each sharing a leaf.

The open pages showed three sigils. Cait could only barely remember drawing them as if they'd come out of something so far beyond herself that she could never touch it, an unstoppable font flowing through her. Her blood was a bursting river under her skull now.

The queen pointed at the first sigil, a word without a sound. "These are the three syllables of my god's name. Our god's name, Cait."

The blood-red nail touched the ink, and Cait could swear she heard the snap of static and smelled ozone. The fingertip traced the figure, one that must have had a start and stop, but Cait couldn't remember either.

The queen pronounced the first syllable, and Cait surrendered. The word was never meant to be spoken aloud, never meant to be pronounced. She had no idea how it would sound until it hit her with the force of a shotgun blast. It was real, all of it. The broken and smoking mirror, the walker between, the ripple causing the stone. She couldn't bear the weight of that knowledge alone, and even with the queen beside her, Cait forfeit all of her strength and passed gratefully from being awake into something else, something black and quiet and comforting.

༒

Someone must have carried Cait to the car because she woke up in it. Everything was submerged and watery, more than just the spattering rain on the windows that made the city lights melt into bubbling constellations that drifted from one instant to the next. The air itself had changed, the atmosphere heavier. Something huge loomed outside, boxed brackets like the bare bones of a skeleton, all corners and height. It stood out against the yellow fog, and she realized it was an electrical tower, taller than anything she could imagine. It reminded her of the moon from the car when she was a child: big enough that it seemed to have always been there.

She watched it as they headed south, toward the yellow lights of the industrial sprawl always on the wrong side of the river.

The queen sat beside her, reading her book, tracing the words with a ruby fingernail.

༒

They passed through a row of headlights, cars parked facing each other to form a processional corridor of mismatched profiles and burning eyes like a gauntlet of mechanical dreams. Reflected light bounced off the rain-wet metal, and everything looked oily and newborn in that. Through the windows, Cait could see kids dancing between the cars, radios tuned loud and to twenty different stations, but all of the songs were pounding and mean.

"When we come out, tell them to make the change," the queen whispered. Her dress had changed again. Even in the stillness of the car, it seemed to flow, driven by an external current as if underwater. She didn't look up from the book.

Cait feared asking why, afraid and trying to remember what she'd even written or thought she had. The page turned, and Cait watched the queen's hand, not the writing in the book. Her fingers worked on something invisible while the index pointed in study.

"Yes, Queen." Alondra's recognition was clipped.

The car rumbled through the corridor, and Cait looked around. Past the rain streaks and headlights, she could see more towers in the distance. The pylons became a row of giants slumped in a march to the sea and maybe beyond, to the depths within it. A tangle of junk ringed the space around them, a midden barely visible in the windblown bonfires placed with purpose.

As the queen's Mercury passed, engines revved, and cars pulled away, kids and No Tomorrows soldiers sitting on the hoods and hanging out of windows. White or Latino or Asian, they were all one in the firelight. This was a party, a big No Tomorrows party, and there was no other like it. A family reunion with gasoline and boom boxes and free liquor. The cars pushed out into a ring, spaced between the bonfires. Lights flashed in a semaphore that Cait couldn't understand.

And they did it all without a word, as if they'd been born knowing it.

The Mercury stopped as the queen closed the book, lingering on the last page. Cait knew that writing to be automatic nonsense. She had been half-blasted out of her mind on that super vodka. No one was supposed to read it that far, much less take it seriously. But the queen had, and she'd found a terrible meaning and purpose within it.

Cait found herself stuck in a loop now, images of the stone and the mirror surface breaking, both giving birth to one another on a Möbius strip hanging here in time. She found the presence of mind to bite down on her cheek, and the jolt of pain ripped her from the trapping thought. Everything resolved into a tighter focus now.

"Ah, you're back with us. That's so wonderful." The queen's eyes filled with something more than respect now as they looked at her. Devotion? "And I thought that I knew all there was to know. But I was so wrong. And you, Cait, have been the one to complete the picture for me."

"I was just—" There wasn't even a word for it, for being outside herself, a conduit.

The queen hugged her tight, and Cait couldn't escape from that nor wanted to.

The music went from cacophony to static for a moment. The queen rolled the windows down, and the rain came in, warmer than Cait had expected. Random noise buzzed for a moment and slowly resolved itself into echoing clarity.

"—ght there's something special on KXLA from a band calling itself Dreamless."

The queen looked out over her people and listened as the voice got stronger, amplified through car speakers and radios large enough to be tombstones. More than that, it echoed throughout the city around them. Who knew how many listeners tuned in to that station tonight?

"Enjoy," said the disembodied DJ as the wet wind surged.

The first strains of an urgent guitar came on, like a lover holding back to last all night.

Ariela opened the door fully and slid out like heavy smoke. "Come on now, Cait. It's time to find out how right we are."

She swallowed the bit of blood that had been rolling around in her mouth, the taste nothing like in her apartment with Tácito's death.

Had that been a week ago? Yesterday?

She put her hand in the queen's and slid across the bench seat. As she emerged into the rain, the kids cheered, their own voices insubstantial and drowned against the building guitar line. What human sound could stand up to that?

It was like standing in an animal's breath, warm and close. Every bonfire in the place flickered in time, pushed down by the wind only to roar back up. Everything in the moment connected somehow intimately to the queen who played the crowd and the wind as a conductor with only the smallest possible motions and maybe even just with her eyes.

Alondra stood next to Cait but watched her sister. She didn't even blink in the rain.

Metal bones ringed the ceremony, milagros cast by an entire city of titans. Cait could see individual pieces in the flat, yellow flickering: differentials, bumpers, crushed automobiles, and even train cars, like everything was declared useless and crumpled into walls of garbage. It was the old world being put to burial.

And the queen would cast the first shovelful of dirt.

Ariela walked without motion to the center of the circle being described by the bonfires and the cars and the reflection on thousands of pieces of jewelry and knives being worn by the kids. She stopped before the fire burning at the center of the circle and thrust her hand into it. A gasp of admiration rose from the crowd as her hands lingered in the embers, finding the perfect one.

Clutched in her cool, soft hand, the queen held a piece of metal, burning with a magnesium-white flare, and lifted it overhead. Sparks rained off her head and bounced down past her as from an incinerating crown.

"Tonight, my brothers and sisters of No Tomorrows, tonight we bring shadow and silence to this world!" Her features were scratched out, stark and appearing to consist only of bone. The datura tattoo on her chest swelled with her inhale. "¡Sombra y silencio!"

"¡Sombra y silencio!" came the reply from the gathered.

Alondra said nothing, though her lips moved. Cait wondered if it had just been lost in the clamor. She found herself wanting to call too, to show she belonged.

The queen threw the ember high into the air, and it finally landed an arm's length from her, gravity dilated sickeningly for a moment. There the ground burned, and fire shot away like a serpent uncoiling. Cait traced it with her eyes, turning her body to keep sight of the spreading flame. It burned with many colors, red coruscating into green and to orange and purple but never for long, barely enough time to think of their names. The flame raced as the music from the radios pulsed in synchrony.

Cait turned in place as the circle traced out, and the etching flame turned inward. The kids whooped and hollered, going counterpoint to the beat, dividing it within itself. The flame split into two, each racing opposite directions but only for a second before splitting again into four and then eight. By now, it was impossible to see the whole thing unfold.

Prismatic light boiled from the floor of the industrial yard as the martial drums came in and built. A collapsing roar bellowed as the fire had nowhere else to divide and grow into, so instead it gushed upward in a sheet. The crowd's reverence nearly knocked Cait over as all the voices made the same sound at the same time, and the first movement of the song ended to a blast of wind. The spreading flame and bonfires were snuffed, and even the headlights snapped out.

A woman's voice started from the radio in glossolalia, soft and infant-toned. The colored flame returned, burning in a shape that Cait knew, the Seal of the Smoking Mirror, though she could have seen the whole only from climbing to the top of everything and looking down. The final traces of color stripped from the flame, and it seethed white now, smokeless and clean.

There came no applause for the queen. It had stopped being a party and was now strictly ceremony. She stood at the center of their focused adulation, ringed in the white glow of the capillary lights at her feet.

TOOM! TOOM TOOM TA TOOM!

Drums thundered from the synchronized speakers, loud enough to make the puddles of rain dance in an earthquake of rhythm.

Ariela nodded to Alondra, waiting for the signal. Dancers melted through the ring of fire and around the queen. Matching the rhythm, they ignited gouts of fire from aerosol cans, flames dancing all around them. Cait could only watch the color and light.

"My family! Let us take a moment to honor the woman who has brought us this gift!" Her hands gestured to Cait and went through some curling motions, echoing the undulation of her black underwater dress. "Honor her vision!"

The crowd paid reverence in long vowels and more spouting flame from the dancers. Cait couldn't help but feel pride at this, different than any other she'd felt. Not even when the queen herself had spoken with approval of her work did her heart swell up in her chest so that her ribs felt too tight.

This is for me. And every fake that I made feels like trash not even fit to burn. Every dope I conned and every dollar I made was worthless.

But this is real.

She blushed all the way down her chest, hot with it now.

"Honor her."

Cait couldn't even smile, only surrender to the adoration that belonged to her, for now she had an audience. She had the ear of the queen and the love of her subjects, and whatever came now was *not* bigger than her because it had come from her. She *was* this big.

"Honor her . . . sacrifice." The queen's words came in the absence of all other sound. The dancers stood still, the rising smoke from the sigil that burned at the center of the yard the only motion.

That and Alondra's hands around Cait's own. They gripped as firm as time, gentle but without possibility of escape.

Cait struggled and could move but only to a certain length. Past that and she was held tight.

"Don't fight this," Alondra warned.

Two other kids, boys as tall as Alondra and decked out in denim and loose leather vests freckled with pins and buttons, took Cait's hands from Alondra, one for each. They didn't leer or smile but accepted their duty with the solemnity of the believer, doubt an unthinkable luxury.

"But . . . the gift!" Cait shouted.

"The gift is yours, dear Cait." Not sorrow nor anything else marked the queen but envy. "You will complete the circuit once it is opened. And you will come to know such things that I cannot even express my desire to switch places with you."

"Then do it!" Cait pulled against her captors, but like knocking over City Hall with her bare hands, it was without effect.

"Someone has to open the window. Someone has to see this through."

"You miserable bitch!" Cait spat.

That got her a slap across the face, not enough to cause damage but certainly a correction. Alondra's glare bored through her.

"Don't say anything more."

"Make me."

Alondra went across the other cheek this time. Both burned from it, where moments ago it had been pride's blush.

"¡Basta!" The queen's voice cut across the yard. "There is no more time for this." Her fingers snapped like a child's back breaking. "Bring her. Let her accept the gift even if she does not want it."

The song rose and fell, waves smashing against an unseen shore. They dragged Cait until she could catch her heels on a rock and stop. Alondra rolled her eyes and hissed at the captors, so they lifted and swung Cait in place, now leaning forward and unable to slow herself further.

Cait saw something else in Alondra's face, something eating at the edges of her confidence.

The queen conducted the crowd and its energy, entering a dance made beguiling by the rippling of her dress and her hair coming undone. She became wild in a way Cait couldn't have imagined moments ago, not even with her fit in the club. That had been submission. This was dominance. All restraint was now abandoned, thrown on the pyre of ceremony as fuel for whatever came next. Lit from below, she seemed to grow huge, her black dress catching the light and becoming a flag of unknown power, claiming this territory for its own.

A sound rolled over all of them, but this wasn't the radio. This seemed to come from within and resonate with every piece and person in the yard. Cait felt it in her bones, a slow hum. The boys holding her hesitated for an instant as it hit, and she wrenched her left arm away and free.

"Hold her!" Alondra yelled, but her voice shook, sounding distant. She felt it too.

Cait swung her left wildly and tried for the knife still in her hidden pocket, but she was held up again, without incident or success.

The sound surged again, this time rearranging all of Cait's guts like tarantulas running through them. It penetrated every part of her in a kind of absent violation.

One of the boys holding her gagged and threw up but didn't relinquish his grip.

The queen sang, her unknown tongue mixing with the voice of the radio. Her arms whipped, and Cait could see a flash of the tattoo and the veil above it, eyes rolled back to whites now and seeing nothing.

Alondra's face pulled taut in worry. She stood two paces away but didn't acknowledge Cait at all.

The queen spat words that Cait wished had no meaning and stood there.

In between phrases of the queen's ritual, the sound rushed in again. It sharpened into something metallic and resonant, as if chains whipped on a steel drum but slowed down such that every individual link was its own tone with echo and decay. Cait felt the sound swim around her but no longer felt sick from it.

The rain came down hard, warm and solid. Still, the sound vibrating through Cait's bones had more substance than the weather. It was the only reality with any weight now. The rest was nothing in comparison.

The queen thrust both arms up with a scream ripped from her. Lightning raked the junk piled around them but without thunder, only a shifting pressure in the air. The tolling sound became the atmosphere, even weather not enough to affect it.

She dropped to her knees, back slumped in exhaustion, breath heaving as she kneeled in what might have been prayer. She said words that only the dirt could hear. The sigil surrounding them all pulsed in time with it, breathing like the tide, ebbing and flowing.

A final sound, this one clearer: a slow, stretched bell tone swarming with overtone and resonances fit to shake the earth beneath them. Cait had felt earthquakes, but this was different, almost inside out.

The queen didn't move but for her hand closest to Alondra and Cait. The fingers curled, except for the pointer, and she slowly raised it to the sky, hyperextending her shoulder as she did.

Cait followed the hand and stared at velvety, yellow-cast night sky. Streaks of silver flew past her, but they weren't rain. They stretched and extended and joined in a patchwork of irregular triangles, stressed and distorted. Something pushed and pulled the space between the stars and tattered clouds like heat-softened steel, working it into something new.

The silver glowed to white, and Cait felt the hair on her arms and the back of her head stand up. The smell of burning insulation or hair swarmed up against her, inside her, as the lattice in the sky curved and pushed inward against some unseen force.

Before it snapped, there sounded a brief sucking of air as the rain and smog over the city was pulled through this aperture now screamingly open between two places. Voices poured through it, hopelessly murky but with a slowed cadence that Cait could recognize as a kind of speech.

The queen dragged herself to her feet and shouted in triumph, syllables without language, only inflection. Gray mud streaked her face and matted her hair, but she didn't care. She had eyes only for the now opened window. The edges of it pulsed with the fading light of the sigil, seeming to draw strength from the other's failing.

Alondra screamed something in response, but there was no triumph there, only anxious fear. The queen had no ears for it.

A breath coughed out of the sky as if some whatever on the other side had tasted our air and found it foul. Mist and vapor coalesced around the edges, purple and blue and black all darkly saturated. The titan murmurings stopped, only to return in a long and astonished shout.

Her captors let go in an effort to escape the sound, and Cait did the same, unable to do anything but cover her ears. That helped but not enough as the sound echoed through everything. She saw that most of No Tomorrows was doing the same, totally overwhelmed even past reverence and into utter submission.

All but Alondra and the queen. Cait saw Alondra shout something to Ariela. Without a word, she turned away in disbelief but not shock. She said something, and Cait had to hear it.

Her blue eyes smoldered as she spoke. "Sabía que Tácito no estaba solo. Pero no creí que estuveria contigo, Alondra."

Alondra and Tácito worked together? The queen knew but didn't try to stop her? Cait's head swam at the thought. Alondra's eyes went wide and wet with sorrow tempered on anger. "¡Tienes que parar esto!"

Her refusal was terrible to see, all envy and defiance that pulled her features to a mask. "¡Nunca!"

Alondra passed her hand in front of her face, fingers curled tight against her palm, and gestured at Ariela. A shimmer in the air, like heat waves, flowed between them and passed over the queen to no effect.

"Te enseñé solo trucos!" she said. "Trucos inútiles que no me podrían hacer daño." Her fingers bent, boneless and impossible, and Alondra reeled as if struck with a ball-peen hammer between the eyes.

A wave of pressure surged from the aperture, and the lattice burned in afterimage on Cait's eyes. The queen boasted of having taught only tricks, that what she herself knew was terrible by comparison. When Cait's vision cleared, she saw something in its place. Violet and ruby starbursts shook out of her vision, and the image came into focus.

Huge eyes hung in the air, exposed and lidless, riddled with veins, maps to unknowable lands. She wanted to scream but didn't have the breath for it. She could only watch: it was not many eyes but only one, appearing as if looked at through a compound mirror that shifted and turned, a kaleidoscope of video feedback, cameras turned upon themselves with the image curling away into somewhere else. Organic and fractured angles of the image overlapped and went from obtuse to acute as the eye darted from place to place.

Its irises were cobalt and deep.

No, wait.

They were brown and even violet. The composite wouldn't hold. Multiple eyes overlapped maddeningly, and writhing nimbus surrounded all that, a perpendicular halo of vapor. Beneath the dust, Cait saw flashes of what looked like metal but woven somehow. The whole of it slithered, uncountable, slowly coming together in unison.

Struggling to her feet and drenched in sloppy mud, Alondra grimaced then spat, "¡Si no puedo salvarte, yo salvaria la familia!"

The queen laughed now. "¿Salvar de qué? ¿La verdad?"

The queen didn't want to be saved. She served a higher truth, one that superseded even family.

The tendrils grafted to one another in clumps, individual pieces surrendering to a larger whole, each taking its place and forming three appendages that moved bonelessly but with purpose. It felt the air and its new environment and reached around.

With every motion, clouds of vapor trailed behind it as if it slowly burned, just too dumb to feel the fire. The myriad eyes looked all in different directions, flickering as if in deep dream. As the feelers, now thick as a man's arm, pushed forward, the eyes followed them, moving in a new unison, maybe understanding now.

The children of No Tomorrows were screaming. Some of them looked to the sky and their new god, but many simply tried to escape. They fumbled in shrieking ecstasy through the mud, reaching for cars or a place to hide in the shadow of the towering junk. Hands slapped against metal and car doors, seemingly forgetting how to operate them and only adding to the manic rhythm.

The queen pointed up and laughed. There, a new sun hung in the sky, a night sun. It cast only shadow, and those seven-lobed eyes swam at its center, each an individual yet shared somehow. The metallic strands held their halo shape, and the three limbs continued to taste this new world, two in the sky and one reaching down toward the ground, toward the three women at the center of the whirling storm.

Cait watched, entranced, and realized only too late that this arm came not toward the queen or Alondra but toward her. Alondra had a hand inside her vest and pulled it out, cold steel gleaming now, not a knife but a gun.

"¡Sí! ¡Terminarlo!" the queen shouted with a child's glee.

Cait registered the words only dimly as the tendril seemed to whip past her. She felt a sudden and painful tugging along the back and side of her head, bringing her to her knees. The weight of the thing pulling on her hair made her flash to images of her scalp being ripped free. Her hands darted into her jacket without thought.

She then saw the light from Alondra's muzzle flash, sharp orange stabbing and flame leaping from her fingers.

"¡Atrápala! ¡Cierre este circuito! ¡Cierralo y—*NGAAH!*" The queen's command to her god melted away into a grunt of shock and pain.

A gunshot followed closely, loud as a whisper in a hurricane's eye.

Cait tried to square the loss of sequence but couldn't. It was just how things were now: consequence preceding action, time itself coming undone.

Ariela reached out, and Alondra groaned as if struck in the stomach, doubled in agony. The gun fell loose.

Cait's fingers closed on the knife's handle, and she wrestled with it, trying to keep to her feet as the thing held her. It wasn't trying to pull her head off, instead yielding to the counter pressure and simply . . . feeling the hair that it had caught. Cait looked back at the gleaming gold and purple-dusted limb as it grasped. It clung but did not constrict. The metallic umbilical led back to the watching eyes, fragmented in a malformed honeycomb prison.

It wanted her, but it didn't know why. It was just exploring.

She pulled the knife free, still sheathed. Her fingers struggled against the slippery leather. From water or sweat, she couldn't tell.

The thing pulled, and Cait had no choice but to take two stuttering steps along with it, closer to the eye, closer to the aperture.

She pulled the sheath free, nicking her left index finger across the first knuckle. At first, she didn't even feel it, but then there was the unmistakable gush of pain before the blood.

The thing held tension, but length flowed from it. The coil around her hair stayed in place, but the tip of the tendril grew so as to better grab Cait all the way around her waist.

Fear boiled in her as she realized she couldn't cut the coil itself. Her arms just weren't long enough and couldn't bend backward. Knowing this, she brought her swing inward and pulled against the thing, craning her head and neck against the pressure as hard as she could, like falling uphill.

Then she sliced with the knife, cutting the hair that the thing held. She heard only a whisper, and the pressure ceased, replaced by forward momentum. With a gasp, she caught herself on one knee in an awkward lunge into the filthy water and litter of purple hair at her feet. The right side of her head felt awash in cold now, but she was free.

The queen cried again as Alondra vaulted upon her. Blood streaked Ariela's face now, but if it was from the bullet, it had only just grazed. The two were bound up in each other, sharing a fate meant for only one.

The torrent of reverberating sound slapped Cait across the face. It came from the hole in the sky and not the thing itself, pressing like a howling wind.

Alondra pinned the queen and just held herself against the wave. Ariela thrashed but couldn't escape, nor could she seemingly work any magic, fingers interlocked with her sister's. Her eyes alternated between careless rolling and a fixed burning on Alondra. Cait stood against the wave and gripped the knife furiously, looking for a target.

The probing arm snaked toward her once again, realizing itself empty-handed. The tip of it unfolded and unfolded again into digits topped by digits topped by digits until so small that Cait couldn't see them, but she knew they extended all the way down to the spaces between atoms. They didn't wiggle chaotically but moved in sequence, hypnotic in its precision.

Cait slashed across her body and caught the thing in mid-lash. The point left a purple streak in the air, holding an afterimage like a waved sparkler in a child's eyes. The image didn't fade even as the thing snapped back, having felt that blow. No shriek emerged, only an organic motion of curling away from heat or pain as an invertebrate might. But just for a moment, for the tendril grew new fingers, multiplying them wildly where it had been cut but without order now, only a geometric increase born from spastic reflex.

Ariela cried and wailed, no reason in it.

"¡Para esto!" Alondra pleaded. "¡No es demasiado tarde!" Her voice rose to desperation. Her twin nooses hung wet and heavy from her shoulders. She couldn't see the tendril curl back upon itself and head toward her.

Cait didn't shout to warn her. "Ariela!" she screamed instead.

And in that moment, she knew that she would choose Ariela at any time. The queen was her patron, her defender. The queen was the woman who had made her work real, more than any other thing ever had. The queen believed in Cait, so she herself didn't have to. She abandoned the moment to that feeling and ran to save her.

But even the queen couldn't be allowed to do this. Even on the basis of faith and love and everything else.

First things first.

Ariela sobbed, and the sound of it rent through Cait and her sister both. Alondra's face went ugly with triumph tempered in loss.

The tendril struck, wrapping itself around Alondra's waist and lifting her off, pulling until the weight of their linked fingers and Ariela herself made it impossible. The thing slackened as if exploring this new resistance. The seven eyes moved as one, focusing on this new toy it held.

"¡No! ¡No puede ser tu!" Her face went to horror and fear. "It is wasted on you!" Ariela's screams melted toward chaos. She yanked back, not letting go, pulling against the god of her own creation.

The winds flayed now, carrying trash and water up from the surface of the industrial yard. They sucked inward, toward the aperture like a massive breath being drawn.

Whatever loomed on the other side, beyond the thing, intimated a reality both terrible and abyssal, depths that couldn't be contemplated much less plumbed or felt out. And every moment the window stayed open, the more that the other side grew accustomed to the taste of this world. With every second, its hunger grew. Cait could feel it now, an intensity and focus radiating from its glare.

It wanted to know this world and didn't care how that knowledge came about. The two free tendrils tasted the metal and trash surrounding them. They reached into a stack of auto bodies with the same ease that the thing that had been Rico had reached into Fellowes's skull. But their passing was marked by violence, wrecks ripping into tatters that rained down on the stupefied children who still remained.

A car pulled away from the industrial rain, and one of the feelers followed it, pushing through the window and wrapping upon itself until it occupied the entire volume of the car before it burst. Then the thing used its fingers to study the debris.

It learned by smashing and studying what remained.

"I was chosen! Solo yo!" Ariela screamed now.

Alondra couldn't answer as the thing had wrapped around her entirely, up to her mouth.

The aperture widened, and behind the swirl of vapor and broken space, there stretched a cathedral. Structures that echoed one another in recursion pulsed and dilated. If there existed a great machine at the heart of the universe, Cait knew it was there. Pieces without name or conception moved in a multiplicative clockwork, forcing the window open even further. Space groaned in the air above them as the machine exposed itself. Gears moved, and they flickered into substantiality.

It had to be reversed. The ripples would die out, but their source had to be cancelled before that could happen. Or *un*happen.

Cait braced herself and held the knife in the air before her as she tried to recall the three names. Hearing the first syllable of these had blacked her out hours ago, but somehow, she'd written them without harm. She had to do it again.

She blacked her mind and wished she'd had some of that Russian rocket fuel, not just herself and the knife that could cut atoms.

She drew the outer border of the first name in an unwavering circle that sparked blackout violet at its edge. Then she sliced and cut, removing anything that wasn't the sigil and adding to anything that was. She let the scene around her pass through, all of the moans and sighs of depressurization, all of the smells of shit and grease and rust, all of the warm rain that felt more of biology than of weather. She let it pass through her and drew the final stroke.

A low bell tone resounded in her guts like a bass double tuned down with her belly right up against the speaker column, vibration to flesh. Where it met the howl of the door between worlds, there came the crash of unmaking.

Ariela turned from her god and her sister's grasp to stare at Cait in astonishment. Her eyes were wide as if now seeing the bottom of the well she was falling into, seeing finality.

"No puedes—" Her voice was a whisper that screamed on the same frequency as the open window in the sky. But she couldn't let go of her sister, not without giving up her prize. She had only her words to stop Cait.

Cait stared at the first name. Written in the air, it didn't waver. She didn't allow herself any triumph and instead started writing the second. This one required more effort, as if pushing through water. Each motion had to be more deliberate, more forced, for the same effect. She emptied herself to memory. She had only seen the sign an hour ago, so it would be fresh if she let it happen.

The queen shouted something in a language that Cait didn't recognize. A wave of grease-streaked water smacked her in the face but didn't knock her over. She was weak, whether by circumstance or choice in animating the window didn't matter. It wouldn't last.

The sign flowed from the white obsidian with the ease and grace of automatic writing, unrestrained by the rational and instead drawing energy from a place before words. Cait twisted her wrist to make the line lay correctly and finished the second, feeling crushed as if at the bottom of a lake, despite the smoothness of motion. She breathed heavy.

She allowed herself a look at the second but dared not speak it. Through the burning in the air, she saw Ariela, seemingly imprisoned in a cage of bent neon tubes. The queen's awful glare burned as she let go of one of Alondra's hands and reached toward her veil.

Cait didn't know what lie beneath it and didn't want to.

Alondra slipped back, only anchored by one point now. The groping tendril pulled back lazily, and the eyes still watched with intent. Its other arms encircled the yard, stretching and extending, following the outer border of the sigil that the queen had drawn in fire. Within these bounds, the ground vibrated and hummed, and gravity seemed lessened.

"Cait! ¡Mírame!" She softened then, inviting with her eyes. "Know my truth."

But Cait still had to work under duress. She made the first stroke and then made the mistake of flicking her vision back to the queen.

With her free hand, Ariela threw aside the black intricacy of the lace veil that had covered her face. Cait stared and couldn't look away.

Ariela's lips were laced shut with thread, black as rain pools on the street, in four black *X*'s. Cait flashed back to her first meeting with Alondra, but those had only been paint or marker. These were real, pressed through flesh and with what must have been excruciating pain.

Had she done it herself?

This was the only thought that came to mind. Not how she'd spoken all this time or when she had done it. But had she committed this act of devotion herself. And she must have.

Alondra struggled against the grasp, trying to free herself with the one hand, but it was useless, like wrestling a bent girder. The gold and copper surface shone as it flexed, uneven and hammered.

"You can't stop me. You can't stop this."

Cait couldn't shut her eyes and see the lips not move as the queen spoke. They didn't even struggle against the stitching.

She could work though. She started the twisting second stroke that marked the defining feature of the third name, the third name of the thing pushing its way into our world.

"I won't let you stop this. I've worked too hard, Cait. I waited forever."

Ariela released her sister, and the tendril resumed its crawl back to the aperture, trailing dust and smoke in its gleaming wake. The queen ran toward Cait, crossing the space between them in her dress of tattered coal. She ran, drifting like smoke, before leaping.

Alondra choked out a gasp of pain and relief as the tendril dropped her and followed along only a step behind the queen.

Ariela's arms wrapped around her, strength through desperation and something like love. Cait could feel it. The queen needed her. This wasn't something she could have done alone, and now that they stood on the precipice of it ending, the queen needed her to *let* it finish, to *let* the event unfold, whether the ripple birthed the stone or the reverse. It didn't matter.

Cait wanted to surrender to it, to let herself make something real. She'd failed so often before, never given anything life. But the truth of this thing was too destructive, too much to be contained. Whatever power she and Ariela had tapped together, it was more than this world could take.

Alondra's eyes lolled, Cait saw in a flash. They rolled as she was brought close to the god and the machine behind her, to the countless echoes of a device that Alondra could scarcely imagine much less be forced to watch. She gasped on the cold and wet but didn't see as the tendril reached around Ariela and Cait both.

The queen smiled beneath her stitching as both lifted, weightless in the god's arm. The ground fell away, and Ariela's hands came across Cait's cheek.

"Yes. This way, we will both know. Both of us will become its children. The Black Rock!" she shrieked, wielding it as a name of power.

They weren't being crushed, but they both would be drawn into it.

Ariela's eyes remained cold and abyssal with depths that no human could contain. They latched onto Cait. "Both of us. Free to finish the work."

Cait was trapped. The ground lay only feet below them still as they were dragged to the eye and the window and whatever waited beyond, whatever devices pulsed at the center of this storm, feeding the god and driving her appetite into the only world Cait had known until now.

She wasn't sure she could pay the ransom that freedom would demand. Her work lived and the queen in that. She couldn't have both.

Cait shook her head as she looked sadly into the eyes of Ariela, lost now. They'd come to this together, but Cait wouldn't accept it. More than even her sister's rejection, this shattered Ariela, let her realize that she'd always been shattered, always been incomplete.

The composite eyes grew, and its oppressive attention rained harder than summer heat. They rose now as Cait thrust the knife into the limb where its substance fell away almost without effort. The cut was uneven in hesitation, but the limb couldn't hold the both of them afterward.

Cait let herself fall away, feeling the strength of the thing melt off her right side.

Ariela screamed as the realization hit her like an imploding skyscraper. The moment surged toward an ending. It would end. There would be no ripples, only stillness.

Cait fell to the ground with an idiot grunt and clambered to her feet, running back to the sigil in the air. It could be finished in two strokes, but she would have to complete them backward now. No time. No time left.

The queen's voice rose but diminished as she came closer to the hole in the world. The rim of it seethed and turned as the final tendril reared back for strength.

Cait summoned up the image and closed her eyes, trusting only herself as she had when she first drew the sign. But inverted now, she performed not an act of creation but one of willful unmaking. Something in the atmosphere resisted, pressing back lead-heavy, as she pushed the sign into being. She felt the whole of it flare with cold flame, anti-heat burning her exposed skin. The welt burned too, giving her urgency.

If the thing made a sound now, it was chaos, removed from tonality and rhythm, only prickling as the smoke and dust from the aperture solidified and fell to the ground, now frozen and locked in time.

Ariela clung to the tendril, hanging only a body's length from her apotheosis. She reached toward the surface of the eye, her ruby nails scratching at the surface and marring the jelly there. Paralyzed, the thing didn't care. Even the last arm stuck, held fast to the air, locked in a pose of attack.

The aperture quieted, settling itself, no longer struggling to stay apart but now thrust wide open.

Cait raised the knife and razored it across the name in the air, the name of the god of No Tomorrows. It was complete and made real.

The black rock that fell into the mirror pool. The black rock that caused the ripple that birthed the rock. Cait saw where the loop could be severed and cut it savagely. She destroyed her work with a stroke.

The bottom half of the name hung for a moment, a slashed banner, before gravity resumed and brought the pieces down. Three semicircles remained, glowing iridescent purple, but the lower hemispheres fell. The circuit was broken and useless now.

Behind her, the thing let out a low moan but not lower than that of Ariela who was now clawing frantically at her god, tearing out great runnels of jelly and marring the iris closest to her. She clawed past the irises and into the eyeballs themselves. The black swelled, liquid ran beneath her fingers until they were covered in it, and then her hand.

She shrieked not in frustration or rage now but in fear. Ariela swung her body and the tendril moved only slightly but perceptibly.

Around the thing made of eyes, the aperture contorted, rough circle increasing in complexity, loops forming on its circumference and passing to shapes without name while colors that no human had seen rippled like a school of extinct and luminous fish.

The whole thing went out of focus for a second, the edges of the window passing into insubstantiality. The border of our space and the other space tightened for a moment, the circle becoming perfect and the thing lurching forward, trying to tear itself free. Everything in sight shuddered, and the towers of garbage danced with palsy.

The last tendril reached for Cait at full speed now.

She saw the queen, wrestling herself closer to the black liquid of the eyes, up to her elbows and still not satisfied.

Cait ran her hands through the writing remaining, the incomplete name, trying to scratch it from existence now. Her hands were drunken tingles at the end of her arms but no longer burning. She pushed the pieces into meaninglessness as significant as worms on the sidewalk. She blew, wishing the thing away as if it had never been.

But it had.

Still she wished for it to go.

When she opened her eyes, her hands were streaked with ash but unharmed.

Above her head, the portal went through its changes again, becoming dazzling and byzantine, so overwhelmed in complexity as to fall into chaos.

The edges of it faded to television static, and the static sucked inward at the same time.

The thing expanded, its outer edges reaching the perimeter of the aperture and distorting. Each iris and tendril grew, grotesquely expanding themselves to the size of the rippling portal, but unevenly, in chaos. The thing was being pulled apart, now at the edges of its eyes, the hidden whites revealed for a second before disappearing to whatever was on the other side.

Ariela laughed as she brought her face close enough to the black jelly to kiss it with her stitched mouth. Her empty laugh echoed as the distortion caught her, pulling her every direction simultaneously, her smile at the center of it smeared with the very flesh of the thing she'd made.

They'd made.

The queen stretched thin and flat, spread to a molecule's depth and running to the edges of the aperture, every direction at once until only nonexistence remained open to her.

Something poured from the collapsing portal now, like a necklace of glowing metal, holding its shape only for a moment. Other debris rained from it: perhaps the machine on the other side broke apart, pieces becoming energized in their passing into our world. The sound of the pieces landing made broken music as they fell in a burning rain, and the storm breathed out its last.

༄

One of the remaining towers of scrap metal lurched and crashed to the mud. Cait started awake, finding herself in the back seat of the queen's Mercury, cold and clammy in the predawn light. She was too tired to move and too tired to even think about it. A glint of light shone, and she saw the white obsidian, catching the pink glow from the east. It stuck into the leather next to her, a hand's width of blade showing out of the clean slit.

She lifted her hand and pushed down on the handle, giggling as she did. The blade sank down, and she pushed until the whole of it vanished into the slice cut from the leather. Then she laughed some more.

"I made it disappear."

But it was still there, stuck in the seat. She knew that but didn't think about it.

Cait leaned forward, everything in her made of pain. She pushed at the back door until it rested on its hinge with a complaining sigh.

"You and me both."

She stood, experimentally at first, and though her knees screamed and grime covered her all the way to her hips, her legs worked. She yanked on the passenger door and leaned in, trying the glove box.

"Surely they keep a bottle in here."

Anything would have been acceptable just to dial back the ache, but it was empty of anything other than the pink slip, a battered revolver, and a pair of black velvet gloves, probably fitted for the queen.

She laughed at that.

Where else would they be?

There was nobody else in the yard that she could see. The children of No Tomorrows and the adults who had guided them here were nowhere to be seen. Maybe they'd decided to live up to the promise of their name, but more likely, they'd all left when the party had gone bad.

Tire tracks, gouged out in escape, had all but obliterated any trace of the sign that Ariela had drawn out in flames last night. The stacks of auto bodies and disused metal seemed smaller in the daylight, but maybe they'd all just fallen over in the storm or the visitation or whatever the hell happened.

She went looking for the book to make sure it wouldn't happen again. She thought about the knife buried in the seat and how it wasn't really there.

Gray mud slicked with a rainbow sheen of oil slopped around her feet as she trudged out to the center of the circle where the queen had been standing. But had she even used the book in the ceremony? Cait couldn't recall now. Maybe it disappeared, sucked back through the portal no longer there either. She shook off the chill that hugged her whole right side and turned up the collar. But it wasn't enough.

Something stuck out of the mud, a tight corner, too regular to be a rut or gouge or piece of trash. Those were too curved or too complicated. She crouched down and ignored the starbursts of pain in her joints and pulled the book out of the muck.

The writing on it was masked but not obliterated, the frontispiece still barely visible through the ash-grey smearing, but it wouldn't ever smell like anything other than garbage and solvents.

"¡Oye! ¡Órale!" The voice rolled across the cold and gummy central space of the yard. It was a woman's: Alondra's.

Cait stood and slid mud off the cover as she did. It glopped down to her boots like giant bird dropping.

Two figures walked toward her, both wearing black but one of them filthy. Even through that, her twin-noose hairstyle remained unmistakable.

The man standing next to her was tall and slim with a deep tan, sandy hair, and green eyes. He looked as if he could have been surfing instead of here, more Zuma Beach than crime boss. She figured that others who'd stood in his way had made that mistake as well. He had a foxlike face with an always-ready smile.

"I'm sorry, Alondra," Cait said.

"Talk to him," she replied. "For he is the king."

"Call me Anton." He raised his hand and waved off ceremony. "Finish your business with her, and then we can settle ours." His voice had a Midwestern flatness, one with every other refugee from the dead heart of America who'd moved to LA for the "better things."

Cait didn't like the ring of that. It sounded very one-way. "I'm sorry about Ariela," she said. "I couldn't stop her. And I did . . . this . . ." She waved her hand around, taking it all in and suddenly swamped by exhaustion.

"She would have found a way even without you. She is very determined."

"Was," Cait corrected.

"If you say." Alondra didn't smile, and instead her face went sour, but she said nothing more. "It is over." She raised her hand over her mouth in the familiar gesture. The eyes above the hand were set in dark hollows, maybe from tears, maybe from exhaustion, maybe both.

The king surveyed what was left of the place. "It's garbage, all of it. Who cares if garbage gets knocked over? Not me."

Cait needed to sit down, so she did without explanation. She couldn't even feel the cold anymore. "What are you going to do with me?"

"What do you want done?" he asked back. His eyes narrowed, but the smile stayed buried. The sun came up behind him, and it wasn't hard to imagine a crown resting on his head or the skull beneath it.

Long live the king.

"I want to be left alone." She clutched the book closer to her chest without thought and couldn't look at him anymore. "But you can't have the book.

Fellowes couldn't get it for you and neither could Tácito." Those were names she knew. He'd know them.

The king took a step closer and knelt down. Alondra's sharp inhale was the exclamation mark at the end of the sentence. "The book fulfilled its purpose. I don't need it or want it."

"And what was its purpose?"

"Knowledge. Just like any other book."

"Or a good way to rid yourself of a troublesome employee. Sorry, family member. Who'd outlived her usefulness."

Anton opened his fingers wide. "My hands are clean. And as ghost stories get told about tonight, they'll only see who lived and fear me even more."

"Don't you mean 'us'? As in No Tomorrows?"

He smirked at the suggestion like he was laughing at a train wreck. "You're a sharp one."

Cait wanted to shrug but was too tired, instead wheezing out a laugh. "Will it be good to be the queen, Alondra?" she asked.

"Talk to—" she snapped.

"I asked *you*," Cait's weary reply came back, driven by the will past fatigue, past any pretense of formality.

"I will be a better queen than Ariela. Better than her head in the clouds dreaming." Her chin jutted forward as she took half a step in.

"So much for always being sisters."

Alondra reddened in response, and her fist came up.

Cait laughed in reply. "Go ahead and hit me." She couldn't feel anything else now. "You're not real." Then she pointed at the king. "And you're not real either."

The king stood up. "Keep the car. But hope that our paths don't cross again." He dusted off his hands, though they were already clean. "Your one favor is walking out of here. Don't ask for another."

Cait pointed, but her index remained only half curled from flagging energy. "Don't lose your crown." She giggled at the joke.

She didn't watch either of them walk away.

With the sun now up, the mud warmed and the stink only got worse. Cait sat on the wide running board of the Mercury and watched the cops pick the place over. She looked right through them.

"You gave me a scare last night," Trager said as he loomed over her. "Didn't figure I'd see you in one piece again."

"I told you it wasn't anything I couldn't handle," she said as she tried to pull herself up straight. "Even got a new ride."

"I'm going to pretend I didn't hear that." He tapped the pen on his clipboard in a simmering tattoo.

Cait tried to stand but couldn't. She instead swung her arm like a drunken conductor. "Bunch of dumb kids had a party in a freak thunderstorm. Some of 'em got hurt by falling trash or by climbing where they shouldn't have been. End of story."

The cops picked over junk, but no body bags could be seen. Not even for Ariela.

He cleared his throat, and it sounded like surrender. "You doing my job for me?" He pulled the glasses down his nose a little bit and scratched behind his ear, showing patched elbow pads on his suit coat. "Now where are the shot callers?"

She shrugged, and her mud-splattered jacket creaked with the stuff. "Where do the shot callers go when shit goes down? They cut out." Cait listlessly stood and leaned against the front fender of the Mercury as she did, leaving a smear of ash-grey dust and dirt behind. "You'll never find the old queen."

Trager grunted in dissatisfaction. "You want to tell me why?" The glasses went back up a bit, and his dark eyes were past lying. They were done with it.

"Am I on the stand?"

"Worse, you're talking to a detective."

Cait shrugged. "Fuck it. You won't believe me anyway."

"I once interviewed a ghost on a twenty-one-inch Zenith TV. I'm open."

She couldn't even laugh at it. "The queen wanted the power . . . the abyssal."

"Abyssal?"

"The other. I don't even know what it is. But she found a way into it with a thing I made. Or she made me make. The order is all . . . fucked up." Her fingers made a pantomime of writing in the air. "She used all the kids and the muscle of her whole gang to make it real for a little while.

"My guess is No Tomorrows won't be doing any of the voodoo shit anymore.

Won't need to. Reputation hangs around for a long time, 'specially the scary kind. Maybe they'll just coast on that."

"And stick to real crimes," he added.

"But *those* you can explain away, right?"

He nodded.

Cait wanted to laugh, but there was nothing left to laugh at. Not this morning. But sometime there would be. She craned her neck and looked around the waste and wreck.

The sun glinted off the jagged edges of the trash and totems in the circular yard. The cops would dig and not find anything. The mud would harden to the consistency of a brick, of adobe. Los Angeles was built on the stuff, and it had lasted this long.

Over the other side of the snaking concrete of the LA river, the city stuck up like a mausoleum fit for royalty.

But even that wouldn't be enough for her.

Not for Ariela.

ACKNOWLEDGEMENTS

This is an incomplete list. Thanks to Corinna Bechko for being an early reader and convincing me that I'm not crazy. Thanks to Gabriel Hardman for the cover. Thanks to Raul Cardenas for reviewing my Spanish and to Zoraida Córdova for edits. Thanks to Scott Gable for the copy and clarity edits. Thanks to Chris Barrus for all those late-night drives around Los Angeles.

And a debt that can't possibly be paid back to John Carpenter.

Matt Maxwell was born in California, sometime between the JFK assassination and the moon landing. Lived there his whole life. Learned to drive stick shift in the parking lot of the ziggurat that you see in Roger Corman's *Death Race 2000* and went to school where they filmed all those soft brutalist sets in *Battle for the Planet of the Apes*. He's worked in video arcades and think tanks, been an animator, taught sociology, thanatology, and ethnomethodology.

His past writings include work for Blizzard Entertainment and stories in both *Tomorrow's Cthulhu* and *It Came from Miskatonic Univerity* from Broken Eye Books. He's self-published a number of books, both nonfiction/commentary and short/long fiction and was also the writer and publisher of the weird western comic series *Strangeways*.

Sure. He'd love to be on your podcast.

http://highway62press.com
@highway_62
(illustration by Steve Lieber)

BROKEN EYE BOOKS

NOVELLAS
Izanami's Choice, by Adam Heine
Never Now Always, by Desirina Boskovich
Pretty Marys All in a Row, by Gwendolyn Kiste

NOVELS
The Hole Behind Midnight, by Clinton J. Boomer
Crooked, by Richard Pett
Scourge of the Realm, by Erik Scott de Bie
Queen of No Tomorrows, by Matt Maxwell

COLLECTIONS
Royden Poole's Field Guide to the 25th Hour, by Clinton J. Boomer

ANTHOLOGIES
(edited by Scott Gable & C. Dombrowski)
By Faerie Light: Tales of the Fair Folk
Ghost in the Cogs: Steam-Powered Ghost Stories
Tomorrow's Cthulhu: Stories at the Dawn of Posthumanity
Ride the Star Wind: Cthulhu, Space Opera, and the Cosmic Weird

Stay weird.
Read books.
Repeat.

brokeneyebooks.com

twitter.com/brokeneyebooks
facebook.com/brokeneyebooks

CPSIA information can be obtained
at www.ICGtesting.com
Printed in the USA
FFHW02n1458290818
48139278-51852FF